WOLF BITTEN

LUNAR ACADEMY, YEAR ONE

ALYSSA ROSE IVY

JENNIFER SNYDER

Cover Design: Najla Qambar Designs

HOLT

Strands of lights and fake garland still decorated the halls of the Wolf Bitten dormitory. How much longer would this crap be up? I'd hoped the girls in charge of decorating would've taken everything down by now, but they hadn't. I wasn't a Scrooge; I just didn't care for holiday decorations. They made things look cluttered and added a sense of tackiness to a space that had once seemed appealing. Besides, the holidays were over. A new semester had begun.

My lips pressed into a thin line at the thought.

It was strange an entire semester had already passed. I should be proud of myself for having survived, but I wasn't. Just because I'd made it through didn't mean shit. I may have passed my classes, but had I really learned anything? Had I made any progress with what I was?

In short: No.

I still didn't accept what I was fully. It still felt like an endless nightmare most days. And, heading home for the holidays had accentuated that. Even though we were encouraged to go home for the holidays, the depression that settled over me from my short visit home had me questioning why the academy allowed it.

Especially for those in my house.

Wolf Bitten was made up of werewolves who'd been created by being bit, which meant there were a lot of us—me included—that a trip home was difficult for. We weren't like those from Wolf Born who'd been raised in this world of werewolves and supernatural creatures. We were humans who'd been turned. Some willingly and others, like myself, unwillingly.

My jaw tightened. Holidays home were considered optional at the academy, but they weren't when it came to my mom. There was no way in hell Lunette Taylor would have ever let me skip coming home for the holidays unless the academy deemed it against the rules. Sure, I could've lied. But it would've got me into a whole heap of trouble.

Just the thought of what my mom might have said or done should I have attempted to stay at the academy over break made a shiver slip along my spine. Holidays were her thing. And, she had always been able to tell when I was lying. She should've been born into the shifter world due to her ability to spot a lie from a mile away.

I paused in front of the door to my dorm and lifted my duffle bag higher on my shoulder while I dug in my pocket for my ID card.

"Holt, what's up? You have a good holiday?" Reuben

asked from a few doors down as he closed the door to his room behind him.

Like most of the others in the Wolf Bitten house, he was cool. I didn't know much about him other than that he roomed with Sebastian Holden. Like myself, Wolf Bittens tended to keep their story of how they came to be to themselves.

"Not too bad." I flashed him a grin, hoping it looked genuine. My mood was slightly sour.

He nodded to my duffel as he stepped closer. "Your mom send you back with any cookies?"

My grin widened and a chuckle slipped free. "Hell yeah, she did. Half of this bag is cookies. I told her how much everyone loves the sweet treats she sends. She said she'll send an even bigger package next month, so I'll have more to share with the house."

"Awesome." He tipped his head toward the ceiling and made a small fist pump action before shifting his attention back to me. "Let me know when you're passing those suckers out. I want to make sure I get some." He patted me on the back before continuing down the hall toward the staircase that led through the center of the house.

"Will do." I slid my ID in the door and waited for it to click before I twisted the knob. Walker was sprawled out on his bed with his laptop open and resting in his lap. Wrappers from various snack food items littered the area around him, and there was a pyramid of empty soda cans built on the floor beside his bed.

"Thought I heard you out there yakking," he said as

he paused whatever he'd been watching and glanced at me. "You already get hit up for some of your mom's homemade goodies?"

"Always do." I set my duffle on my bed and sniffed the air. "Dude, it stinks in here. It smells like Cheetos and body odor."

"Considering I haven't showered in a couple of days and Cheetos were the last thing I ate, I'd say your sniffer is on point."

"You're fucking gross." I chuckled and shook my head as I unzipped my bag. I pulled out two canisters of cookies and placed them on our shared desk. My gaze drifted to the window above the desk to see that it was still gloomy outside. "I'm surprised Paris hasn't been by to snap you out of your funk yet."

"She's not getting in until dinner." Walker stretched on his bed until he was able to snag one of the canisters off the desk. "These for me?"

"One is. Not that one, though." I found the one in the bag meant for him and held it out. It had been wrapped in silver paper with little green Christmas trees. "You should've come home with me like I said. All my mom talked about was how much she wants to meet you."

It was true. She'd given me crap for not insisting that he come home with me for the holidays. To her, it was the saddest thing in the world for someone to spend a holiday alone.

Walker's face fell. I averted my eyes and continued unpacking. I knew his reasons for not going home. They were heavy. And, I hated that I'd said anything at all about him opting to stay here instead of returning home or tagging along with me.

"I'd like to meet your sweet mama one day too. You'll have to thank her for the cookies for me," Walker said.

The sound of him popping the canister open drew my attention to him.

"Oh, no. Me thanking her won't do. She'll want you to thank her yourself." I chuckled, knowing it was the truth. "You can guarantee that the next time she calls to check on me, she'll be asking if you're around so she can speak to you."

It wasn't that she wanted to make sure he thanked her for the cookies, but more about her needing to make sure he'd enjoyed them. It was how she worked. My mom was southern, through and through. There was always a fresh pitcher of sweet tea on hand in our house and another dinner plate on standby should someone need to be added to the table. She loved making people happy, and one way she did that was through baking and cooking.

God, I loved her. However, I was glad to be back at the academy.

Since my attack, she'd become more smothering than ever. Probably because there was nothing she could do to fix what happened. She'd prayed for me, though. While I didn't think it had done much good, she sure did. She swore it was her prayers that led me to Lunar Academy. That it had been the answer to them.

I'd be lying if I said I didn't believe the same.

"Holy shit, is this deer jerky? I love your mom's deer

jerky, dude!" Walker shouted, drawing my attention back to him. He tore open the bag and shoved a piece in his mouth, then held a hand out to me. "Give me your phone. I'm calling her right now and thanking her for this awesomeness."

I arched a brow. "Seriously?"

I didn't want him to call her. Not right now. I'd talked to her minutes ago. Even though I was eighteen—nineteen in less than four months—she still made me check in with her when I traveled. It didn't matter that it was only three hours from my tiny hometown to Brentwood and Lunar Academy, she still wanted to know I'd made it safely.

Mom was a worrywart. Always had been.

"Yes. Seriously," Walker said between chews. He shook his hand. "Give it."

I reached in my pocket for it and held it out to him. A low growl traveled up my throat. My wolf shared in my irritation at the situation. It was one of the emotions we shared frequently, if I was being honest.

"Here." I gave him my cell.

Walker tossed another piece of deer jerky in his mouth before scrolling through my phone in search of my mom's number. When he found it, he tapped on her name and placed my cell to his ear before flashing me a shit-eating grin.

"Holt, honey. Is everything okay?" I heard my mom's frantic voice after the second ring. My chest tightened. I should have known she would think something awful had happened due to me calling her again so soon.

"Hey, Mrs. Taylor. This is actually Walker. Holt's roommate. I just wanted to thank you for the cookies and jerky. I really appreciate it. Your deer jerky is my absolute favorite," Walker said.

"Oh, honey. You're welcome. It was nothing, really. I'm just glad you enjoy it." I could hear the smile in her voice.

It warmed my heart.

Even though I found her tendency to be suffocating at times annoying, she was still the best and I loved her.

I resumed unpacking my things.

"Well, I just wanted to call and say thank you." Walker's eyes were on me. I could feel them. It was strange the way things like that were more noticeable now that I had my wolf. I glanced over my shoulder at Walker. He was about to hand me the phone; I could tell. I shook my head, and his grin grew. "Do you want to talk to Holt? He's standing right here, waiting."

I flipped him off before jerking my phone from his grip.

"Hey," I said with a sigh, knowing I'd be stuck on the phone with her forever now.

"Hey, honey. That Walker is such a sweetheart. I'm glad he enjoyed his package. Now, don't forget to pass out those other canisters. And remember, I even made one for whatever girl you have your eye on."

Walker laughed at that. I reached for an empty soda can on top of his pyramid and chucked it at him. It hit him in the chest with a thump.

"I already told you there isn't anyone I've got my eye

on, but I'll be sure to pass the other containers out. One of the guys in the house already asked if you sent me home with anything extra. I told him that you had, and that you also planned on sending a bigger package next month. He's looking forward to it. They all love your sweets."

"I love hearing that!" There was a smile in her voice that had one of my own twisting at the corners of my mouth. "So, what are your plans for this evening?"

My smile died.

"Not much. I'll probably head to the dining hall in a bit for something to eat and then hang out with Walker and his girlfriend some tonight."

"Be sure you go to bed early, though. You know Monday morning will be rough on you if you don't. After all, you did sleep in until almost one in the afternoon every day you were home."

I rolled my eyes, even though she was right—on both accounts—but still. I didn't want another lecture. All I wanted was to get off the phone and unpack.

"I still can't get over how tired you were," Mom said.

"Me either."

I hadn't realized how exhausted I was until I came home for the holidays. It had been nice to catch up on sleep while I was there. There was nothing better than being away from home for a while only to come back and sleep in your bed. I'd been at the academy for months, but the place still didn't feel like home.

It probably helped that my parents hadn't changed a single thing about my room since I left. I wasn't sure how long they'd keep it that way, but I was thankful they'd left it alone for the time being.

"I'll make sure I get to bed early. Don't worry, Mom. I'll talk to you later, okay? I'm going to head to the dining hall for something to eat." I was hungry, but in reality, I'd probably just pop open one of the containers and eat half the cookies inside by myself. Also, Dad had slipped me another bag of deer jerky, so there was that to tap into as well.

"All right, I'll let you go. Have a good evening. I'm glad you made it home safely. Tell Walker I said thank you for calling, and that I hope he likes the cookies too. I mixed it up a little this time." Excitement rang through her tone. "Be sure you check in with me over the next couple of days. I know you don't want to call me every single day. Your dad says that's too much of me to ask, but I wouldn't mind if you checked in at least twice during the week. Let me know you're still alive and how things are going at that school."

That school.

I knew she hadn't meant for her word choice to set me off, but my wolf bristled. Her word choice rubbed him the wrong way too. We were both feeling crabby. I blamed it on not having shifted in nearly three weeks.

The last time had been before I left for winter break. While Lunar Academy was a great place to learn how to be a werewolf and manage that side of yourself, it didn't mean there weren't rules. While I understood the need for them, I hated rule number one most.

No shifting except during school sanctioned times.

Typically, those times were at the end of every season and during full moons. Still, their schedule didn't seem regular enough for my wolf. He apparently needed more time in his own skin.

"I'll call more frequently. I promise," I said, knowing that was what she wanted to hear.

"Good. I'll talk to you soon, honey. Love you."

"Love you, too. Bye." I hung up and flopped on my bed before running my fingers through my hair.

"I don't know why you act like it's such a big deal to talk to your mom. She's a sweet lady," Walker said.

I glanced at him. "She is sweet. I know that. She can just be overbearing at times."

"Duh, she's a mom. Isn't that her job?" He shoved a cookie in his mouth. "I mean, if she's a good mom, it is. We both know mine was shit."

Guilt crashed through me. Every time we got on the subject of parents or homelife, I always felt bad for having a better one than Walker. He rarely said a word about it, but still.

"I know it's her job, and I love her for it. I do. I just... I need something to eat, and honestly, I think my wolf really needs to shift."

Walker nodded, totally okay with me dropping the conversation altogether. "Mine too. You have no idea how many times I was tempted to while everyone was on break." He popped a cookie in his mouth. What did he do all break? "I'm sure they'll let us shift sometime soon, though. Just be thankful for your mom, okay?"

"I am. And, you're probably right about them letting

us shift soon." I sat up on my bed, and popped open one of the canisters trying not to stare at Walker as old memories seemed to twist the features of his face.

Walker's mom had been a shit mom, exactly like he'd said. She left him and his dad when Walker was two. Apparently, she never bonded with him like she should have and decided that being a mom wasn't something she was cut out for.

So, she left.

His dad was a good guy, but he passed away about a year ago. According to Walker, his death was expected. He had pancreatic cancer. Walker had gotten himself turned with the hope of being able to save him. He'd heard stories of our kind and tracked one down. It didn't take him long to find one. Too bad the guy hadn't told him someone as sick as his dad couldn't be saved before passing along this curse. His dad's body was too sick for a wolf to settle and thrive inside him.

He died hours after Walker bit him.

Now he was here, at Lunar Academy, carrying the guilt of not being able to save his dad and being responsible for ending his life sooner than the cancer would have.

While his situation was a hell of a lot sadder than mine, at least gaining a wolf was a choice he'd made. It had been something he'd wanted.

For me, it was anything but.

TORI

I watched the trees pass in a blur as Dad drove us toward Lunar Academy. Mom glanced at me from the passenger seat. She reached around and rubbed my knee. A sad smile twisted her features. Saying goodbye had never been her thing. It wasn't mine either, but I was ready for my second semester at the academy to begin. Heck, I'd been ready since day two of winter break.

Everything about the place fascinated me.

While being home again had been nice, sometime during the last few months, Lunar Academy had become my home too and it had felt strange being away. Not having class or coffee dates with my roommate, Summer, had left me feeling off-kilter. Schedules and living in a routine were my thing. I was a creature of habit. When my routine was disrupted, even for a short amount of time, I felt it dramatically.

It left me irritable, which was never a good thing. Especially during the holidays.

My parents had asked multiple times if I was okay. I'd told them I was fine, that it was just being thrown off my routine making me crabby, but they didn't believe me. I could see the worry in their eyes. It was the same thing in my mom's eyes now.

"Are you going to be okay without me?" I asked her, flashing a smile. I'd hoped my teasing would ease her festering worry. My hand reached out to cover hers, and I gave it a gentle squeeze.

"Of course." Her eyes teared up, and she sniffled. "I get emotional in these situations. You know that." She smiled wide, but it didn't erase the worry from her eyes.

"She'll be fine," Dad insisted. He reached for her hand, removing it from my knee, and brought her knuckles to his lips. "We'll stop by that Greek place she loves so much on the way home. I'll make sure she orders her favorite seasoned lamb dish. Then, I'll take her to that little ice cream place around the corner before we head home." He pulled up to the unloading area in front of the academy and shifted into park.

"That sounds amazing," I said, leaning forward in my seat. A yawn slipped past my lips. "But I think a nap sounds even better."

"I thought you looked tired. Did you not sleep well last night?" Mom asked. She'd shifted around in her seat to get a better look at me.

"I slept like a baby, but I guess I'm still catching up

from the last few months of crazy nights and early mornings here." I nodded to the academy.

Everything I'd just said was a lie.

I hadn't slept at all last night. I'd tossed and turned, worried about my new classes. If I'd like the professors. If I'd be able to keep my grades up. If I'd be able to get my laundry done before class tomorrow morning.

Most of all, I worried about the sanctioned run, which would be happening shortly after returning to campus.

"Want some help carrying your things inside?" Dad asked. He popped open his door and slipped out.

"No. I'm good." I gathered my purse and water from the backseat before climbing out. "Thanks for the ride."

"Oh, honey. You know you don't have to thank us. It's only an hour and a half drive. We're happy to do it. Gives us more time with you," Mom insisted as she exited the car too.

Being so close to home was one of the things I loved about the academy when I first signed up. I'd envisioned coming home nearly every weekend to see my parents and friends from high school, but that hadn't happened. I was busier than I'd anticipated between classes, studying, and the social life Summer insisted I had to have.

I'd tossed another wrench in my plans of coming home on weekends when I decided to sell my car. I'd said it made sense to sell it, so I didn't have to pay the yearly fee to store it in the garage beneath the academy. Another reason was that I'd needed the money to help tide me over until I was able to get a job. I hadn't mentioned that last part to my parents though. They knew I'd been given a scholarship, but weren't fully aware of how much that didn't cover. I had no intention of telling them. They had enough money issues to worry about without me adding mine to them.

Besides, I was perfectly fine without a car. Brentwood, the small town where Lunar Academy was located, was small enough that a person could easily walk anywhere in minutes.

I slung my purse over my shoulder and pulled Mom in for a hug. She squeezed me tight. "I know. I'm going to miss you guys. Love you."

It was the truth. While they weren't my biological parents, they were still my parents in every sense of the word. I loved them immensely.

Mom released me from her bear hug. "We love you too. Make sure you call us, okay? Frequently."

"I will. Promise." I grinned.

"Checking in once or twice a month would be nice. We don't want to smother you," Dad said as he rolled my suitcase from the trunk over to where Mom and I stood.

"Don't listen to him." Mom shoved him playfully. "Call a couple of times a week. I'm not asking to hear from you every day, but two or three times a week would be nice. You can even just text us if you want instead."

I'd never gone a week without talking to them in some form, whether that be by text or an actual phone call, but I didn't say so.

"I'll check in. I promise." I stepped to Dad and gave him a hug before taking my suitcase from him.

Another vehicle pulled up behind ours, and one of the few sets of twins I'd noticed at the academy slid out of the backseat. I couldn't remember their first names, but I knew their last name was Hazel. I'd seen them around campus but didn't have any classes with either of them even though they were first-years like me.

Maybe that would change this semester.

Someone else slipped out of the vehicle along with them. A guy I recognized from my Moon Phases class last semester, Ryan Grayson. He and the girl twin had been together for a while now. I imagined he'd gone home with her for the holidays. For whatever reason, this made me smile. They were cute together.

"I should probably get inside and see if Summer is here yet. She was supposed to get in a little while ago," I said.

Mom wrapped her arms around me for another hug. "Tell her we said hello. Maybe she can come home with you on spring break. We'd love to meet her."

"I'll run it by her," I insisted as I returned her hug.

There was a chance Summer might actually be okay with that. She didn't have the best relationship with her parents, especially not after she was turned.

Dad kissed me on the forehead once I untangled myself from Mom. "We'll talk to you soon. Love you. Hope you have a great last semester of your first year. And, try not to get into any trouble."

"Ha, ha. Funny." I rolled my eyes.

I wasn't a troublemaker. Not at all. I did everything by the book. It was how I'd been my whole life. Schedules and checklists were my favorite. Rules too. Each helped make life a little less chaotic in their own way.

"Never know. You're living the academy life now. You might end up going to some wild party and then finding yourself in trouble. Don't hesitate to call us if you need someone to bail you out. At least then we'll know you've had a little fun while you're here." Dad flashed me a wicked grin as he sidestepped Mom's playful jabs to his ribs.

"Hey. She doesn't need you, Mr. Rule Breaker, giving her any crazy ideas." She shifted her full attention to me. "Don't listen to him."

"I never do," I teased as I started in the direction of the Wolf Bitten dormitory. The Hazel twins and Ryan Grayson had already unloaded and walked away. Since the drive was too narrow for Mrs. Hazel to go around Dad's car, she honked. Another car pulled in behind her. "You guys should probably go. You're holding up the line." I waved them away as I walked.

"Talk to you soon. Love you, honey," Mom said for a final time.

I watched as they climbed in their car and drove off. "Yep. Love you guys, too."

Once I stepped inside my dorm house, I said hey to a few people in the main lounge before making my way up to the fourth floor where the first-year dorms were. Once there, I headed to the end of the hall. The room I shared with Summer was the last door on the left. I inserted my

ID card to unlock the door and stepped inside, lugging my suitcase behind me. Summer sat at our shared desk, painting her toenails. As soon as she saw me, her face lit up with excitement and she hobbled over on her heels to give me a hug.

"Oh my God! I'm so glad you're back!" She released me and flipped her long blond hair over her shoulder. Her eyes focused on my face. "Wait. Are those bangs?"

My fingers lifted to touch them. They were still new enough to have me nervous about other's reactions to them. "Uh, yeah. I wanted something different. Do you think they look okay?"

"They look super cute! I like the way they frame your face." She hobbled back to the desk chair and resumed painting her toenails bright purple. "So, tell me about your holiday break. Was it fabulous? I guarantee you it was way better than mine."

I cringed. Summer's home situation was a complete one-eighty from mine. My parents were accepting of my wolf, because they were wolves themselves. Summer's parents, not so much. They were human and seemed uneasy about the whole werewolf thing. Summer was turned by some jackass boyfriend who got a little rough with her one night. She flipped out when she realized what he'd made her, and went to her parents for help. It had been a bad idea, though. They hadn't known the shifter world existed any more than she had. They took her to a few doctors they paid to keep quiet, but none of them could fix her. Then, they learned about the academy and sent her here to learn more about what she was or if there was a way to fix herself.

Summer's theory was they wanted her out of sight and out of mind. I agreed with it.

I lifted my suitcase onto my bed. "It was good. Fun. Quiet. I enjoyed being home, but it's nice to be back at the academy."

"That's it? Oh, come on. You've got to tell me the juicy details. How did it go with your mom's side of the family? Was there more tension like you thought? Did they treat you okay?"

I unzipped my suitcase and grabbed the bar of salted dark chocolate from the inside pocket I'd tucked away earlier, then kicked off my Converse and flopped down on my bed. The wrapper crinkled as I opened it, and the heavenly aroma of chocolate floated through the air. My mouth watered.

"Eh, it was okay. There was some tension, but I handled it well," I said.

I had. I'd made sure to have a smile on my face the entire time, and to laugh and cut up with everyone exactly like I did every holiday before I'd been turned. Grandma Myrtle seemed irritated with me, but that wasn't anything new. She'd been irritated with me since day one. I didn't think she liked that Mom had resorted to adopting a human child. Or maybe it was that she didn't like the fact Mom had adopted at all.

Who knew?

All I knew was that she wasn't any kinder to me now that I was a wolf than she had been when I was merely human. The only way she'd be happy with me was if I had been born a wolf like her. Like, my mom.

"That's good." Summer wiped the side of her pinky toe with her index finger. "Sucks things weren't better for you. I know how much you wish they were."

She did know. We'd had this talk before I left. I was worried things would be worse with Grandma Myrtle since this was my first time seeing her since having been turned. What I hadn't expected was for things to stay the same.

I broke off a piece of my salted dark chocolate and popped it in my mouth. "Yeah, but it is what it is."

I hoped my words sounded believable. Deep down, I didn't feel so nonchalant about the situation. It bothered me when people didn't like me, especially when they hadn't given me a chance. Ever.

"True." She glanced up at me. "I'm just glad you weren't a kiss ass the whole time to them."

"Nope. Definitely not." I averted my gaze to my chocolate as I tore off another piece.

"Tori..."

"What?"

"We talked about this before you left. You said you weren't going to do that whole people pleaser, kiss ass thing you always do," she insisted.

"I know. And, I didn't. Much."

She rolled her eyes and let out a long sigh. "Next time, you better show some backbone. It's the only way your Grandma Myrtle, and everyone else in your mom's family, will pull the stick out of their asses."

Or it could make it worse, I thought to myself as I chewed.

"So, how was your trip home?" I asked, needing to change the subject.

"Ugh," Summer huffed. "My parents are so normal to me on the phone, but the second we get in a room together, they start to flip out. I can sense it. You know? Their fear and unease lingers in the air around them. Also, I'm pretty sure they slept with their bedroom door locked the entire time I was home, which made me feel super welcome."

My teeth sank into my bottom lip. I didn't know what to say. I felt bad for Summer, but I knew telling her so would piss her off. She didn't like when people pitied her.

"Don't fill up on chocolate. We're heading to the dining hall in a bit. Then, I was thinking maybe we could pop over to Last Call for a few drinks to celebrate."

"What are we celebrating? Starting a new semester?"

Summer gave me a look that said I should know better than to ask. "Surviving holiday break, duh. Well, at least that's what I'm celebrating. Time with my parents is like time spent in hell."

"Actually, I was thinking about staying in tonight. I don't have anything clean to wear since I pretty much took everything I own with me over break and I forgot to wash my uniform before I left." I popped another piece of chocolate in my mouth.

"Um, no." She glared at me. "You're coming out with me. Everyone will be going out for a drink tonight. You know they will. Besides, I already told Paris we'd meet her and Walker in the dining hall."

I paused mid-chew. "I'm assuming Holt will be there too, then."

"Maybe." She grinned.

Butterflies erupted in the pit of my stomach at the thought of seeing him.

I'd been avoiding Holt Taylor since the beginning of the year for reasons I found hard to even explain to myself. He was cute. A southern boy with a charming smile and gentleman-like manners. Exactly the kind of guy I could get too wrapped up in all too quickly. There was something about him that called to me in a way no other guy ever had before.

Not even Danny Fisher, my childhood crush from seventh grade through my senior year of high school.

In short, the reaction my body had to Holt scared me. I'd never had such a strong physical reaction to a guy before. Seeing him smile made my knees weak. Hearing him say my name made my panties wet, and having him accidentally brush against me while standing in line to pay for food was enough to send me into near cardiac arrest.

The guy was freaking hot as the sun, and for whatever reason, he was interested in me. To be fair, I knew I wasn't ugly, but I also didn't think I was his type. I imagined his type to be blond, tall, super tan, and incredibly thin with big boobs. Supermodel pretty. Not mediocre like I was. I was short, small-chested, my skin was creamy instead of tan, and my hair was plain brown and frizzy. There was nothing spectacular about me.

At least not when it came to my looks. I was a plain Jane.

However, if we were talking about photography, I knew I had a knack for capturing amazing angles. Color splashes and nature scenes were my specialty. I loved capturing still shots of nature, but I also found that I enjoyed photographing people lately.

Lunar Academy had some interesting characters—Holt Taylor being one of them.

"So, change out of that frumpy sweater and those leggings into something that says you're ready for some fun instead of lounging around on a couch somewhere stuffing your face with chocolate," Summer insisted as she finished painting her final toenail.

I skimmed over what she was wearing, finally taking notice. She was dressed in a pair of dark skinny jeans and wore a tight-fitting turquoise blouse with a little dip in the front to showcase her ample amount of cleavage. The color was beautiful against her sun-kissed skin.

I broke off another piece of my dark chocolate. "I don't have anything to wear. I brought all my good clothes with me over break. Everything is dirty."

"Borrow something of mine." She gave me a look that said I should already know this, that it was a given. "I bought a couple of new sweaters while I was home. There are also two pairs of new boots in the closet that are both super cute. Feel free to look through them all."

I fought the urge to roll my eyes at the mention of her

purchasing new boots while on vacation. Summer's shoe collection was already out of control. Half of our shared closet was her stackable shoe shelves that nearly reached the ceiling. I was nervous every time I opened our closet doors that something would shift and the entire thing would come toppling down on me.

We didn't have room for her to buy any more shoes, but I didn't say so. It wasn't my place. Everyone had their thing, and shoes were Summer's. Mine was cameras and accessories for them. I had a collection of lenses and straps.

"There's a red sweater I bought that I think would look great on you. It's soft and cable-knit style, exactly like you would normally wear." Summer hobbled over on her heels to the closet and rifled through the contents until she found the sweater she was talking about. She pulled it out and held it up to me. "Perfect. It looks great with your fair skin and dark hair. Plus, it's been scientifically proven that men think women look better when they're dressed in red."

"Why is that?"

"Apparently, they associate red with sex."

My cheeks heated. I wasn't a prude, but I didn't think I wanted to walk into a bar and have any guy immediately think of sex when he saw me. It sounded like a bad situation waiting to happen.

"Try it on," Summer insisted. "I love the back of it. It's super cute, yet sexy."

When she spun it around, I was able to see there wasn't much of a back to it. It was ripped into ribbons, making it look as though someone had taken scissors to it. One-inch strips started at the collar and made their way to the hemline of the sweater.

"You're kidding, right?" I cast her a sideways glare. "How do you even wear a bra with this? It'll show."

"You don't. Problem solved." Her fingers ran along the strips, touching them tenderly. The material it was made of did look soft, I just wasn't sure the style was for me. "Besides, it's a thick sweater. You don't need to wear one with it anyway. No one will see anything."

The truth was: Even if it was a thin material, I could probably get away without wearing a bra with it. I was flat-chested. Incredibly so. Still, that didn't mean I felt comfortable being in public without a bra on.

"I know that look." Summer rolled her eyes.

"What look?"

"The one you're giving me right now. You're not going to wear this sweater unless you can wear a tank top underneath it. And, a bra. At least wear a black tank top with it, okay? Red and black look great together."

I laughed. She knew me so well. We'd only been roommates for a few months, but had already figured out how each other worked. "Deal. I'm also wearing these leggings." I pulled at the stretchy material covering my thigh.

"Good grief. I knew you would say that, too. I suppose you don't want to borrow a pair of boots either? Let me guess, you'll be wearing your scuffed-up Converse instead?"

I flashed her a grin. "Yep."

I tugged my baggy sweater off, revealing the plain black tank top I already wore beneath. Summer rolled her eyes, but didn't say a word. She handed her sweater to me and then hobbled back to the desk chair.

"Let's give my toenails another minute to dry, and then we can head to the dining hall to meet everyone before popping over to Last Call," she said as she fanned and blew on her toes.

I slipped the sweater over my head and marveled at the softness of it. When I stepped to the full-length mirror on the back of our dorm door, I noticed the sweater didn't look half as bad on me as I thought it would. It looked cute. Sexy even.

"That looks great on you! You should keep it."

My gaze snapped to her. "What? No. You just bought it."

"I have loads of clothes. It's just one sweater. Think of it as a Christmas gift."

"Okay. Thanks."

"I think my nails are dry. Ready to go?" Summer slipped on a pair of wedge sandals and grabbed her coat. Her toes would be frozen by the time we made it to Last Call, but I knew she wouldn't care. She was the type who bought into the whole pain for beauty adage. I didn't. Which was why I was wearing Converse and leggings. Comfort was my style.

"Yeah." I slipped my shoes back on and then grabbed my purse. It was chilly out, but the sweater was thick enough that I didn't need a jacket. Especially not after I had alcohol in my system.

My wolf bristled. She was unsettled. Pent-up energy radiated from her. Going out might be a good idea. It might help to settle her. Having a drink might, too.

However, if Holt came, neither one of us would be settled no matter how much alcohol was involved.

The dining hall was packed, but it didn't take long for us to spot Paris, Summer, and Tori. Hell, I would've been able to spot Tori with my eyes closed. Something about her drew me in.

I skimmed over the length of her as we neared the three of them. She was focused on the conversation happening at the table, which let me stare at her for longer than I normally would. Her brown hair was piled high on top of her head the way I liked. It showcased her beautiful, slender neckline. The sweater she wore was snug, hugging her just right, and when she leaned forward in her chair, I was able to snag a glimpse at the back of it. It looked as though someone had taken a razor to it, cutting it into sections. While no skin was visible through it, it still made me think the same thoughts as though there had been. She shifted sideways in her seat and kicked her foot out to retie her shoe. I smiled when I caught sight of her signature shoes—a scuffed up pair of black and white Converse.

The girls laughed at whatever Tori had said. A wide smile spread across her face as she finished tying her shoe and then shifted to sit back in her seat again. Her smile was contagious. It had one of my own stretching across my face as I stepped closer. Not only was Tori beautiful, but she was also a good person. The proof was in the people around her. She'd made friends here that went beyond her assigned roommate.

I couldn't say the same for myself.

Not really. I had people who said hello when I passed them in the halls, but they weren't friends. They were acquaintances. Walker was the only real friend I'd made while here. Hell, he was the only real friend I had nowadays. Period.

Once upon a time, I'd had loads of friends, but after the attack, I let them all go. They'd tried to stay in my life, but the person I was—the person I'd been before—died the night I was attacked. My parents were the only people I carried with me to the other side after.

I split my life in two in that instant—it would always be thought of as before and after. The way things had been and how they were now.

"Hey, babe," Walker said in the weird voice he only used for Paris. It was deeper and much more masculine than his regular voice. I rolled my eyes, per usual, at the sound of it. I still didn't understand why he did it. I'd told him before I doubted she dated him because of his voice. "I missed you so damn much." Walker grabbed Paris's hips and pulled her close. She melted against him in a way that looked easy and effortless.

I crammed my hands into the front pockets of my jeans and shifted my gaze from the two lovebirds to Tori and Summer.

"How's it goin'?" I asked with a slight nod of my head.

"Not too bad," Summer answered. "I'm glad to be back, but I'm seriously ready for a drink tonight. Let's hurry up and get some food." She pushed her chair out and stood.

I nodded, knowing exactly what she meant. A drink would be great right about now.

"Let's migrate that way, then." Tori slipped from her chair, hitching her thumb toward the food.

"Yes. Let's." Summer grabbed Paris's arm and jerked her away from Walker. "Come on. They'll be plenty of time for you guys to make out later. Let's get food, and then we can head to Last Call for drinks."

I was grateful for Summer's hurry to get moving. It saved us all from awkward silence while Walker and Paris made out.

"Whew. I'm so glad it's not meatloaf," I heard Tori mutter.

"You don't like meatloaf?" I asked as I stepped closer to her so that a few people could get by. This place was busy. I was surprised. I figured everyone would still be stuffed from their holiday meals.

Tori wrinkled her nose. She looked adorable when she did that. "I like my mom's meatloaf, but not the academy's. I'm not a fan of the ketchup they squeeze on top before putting it in the oven. It looks too much like blood, and it makes me think of the drinks the Wolf Bloods drink." A disgusted look overtook her face, and even though we were clearly having a conversation, she didn't look at me once.

Maybe it was pathetic, but I'd been hoping to see her eyes.

I'd have to settle for our close proximity, it seemed. While I knew she was leaning in because she worried someone from Wolf Blood would hear what she'd said and take offense, it still excited me to be so close to her.

In fact, parts of me seemed too excited, and I hoped she didn't notice.

I placed a hand in my pocket and carefully adjusted myself while sliding my tray down the buffet, following behind Tori.

"I know what you mean," I said, hoping too much time hadn't passed between when she'd spoken and I'd decided to reply. If there had been, she didn't let on. The pizza called to me. So, I grabbed two slices. "I'm just glad it's not a holiday dinner. I'm sick of mashed potatoes and gravy."

Tori glanced at me, a dumbfounded expression twisting her features. For a brief moment, I thought of what I could have said to make her look at me like that, but really all that mattered was that I could see her eyes now. Her beautiful blue eyes. "I could eat mashed potatoes and gravy every single day of my life. Especially if I had a warm, buttery roll to dip in it."

"You remind me of my mom." I blinked. Why the fuck had I just said that? I wanted to throat punch myself. Oh my God! "Uh, I mean that's her favorite, too. Mashed potatoes and gravy. She loves them."

Tori's cheeks grew pink. Shit. I'd embarrassed her. Great. "Cool," she said. Her gaze slipped to the food in front of her, and the conversation was over. Just like that.

My throat pinched tight. *Smooth move, Holt. Smooth move.*

Tori made herself a salad before grabbing a few slices of bacon. I watched as she crumbled them on top. One thing I'd noticed about her was that her veggie consumption was particularly high for a wolf. At least, I thought so, considering the way our bodies needed protein now. I often found myself wondering if she hadn't been a fan of meat before she was turned.

Had she been a vegetarian? That would suck.

I knew there were some vegetarian wolves at the academy, though. Nadia Hazel was one. She was in one of my classes last semester, and we'd shared the same lunch, so I'd noticed a time or two when she reached for the non-meat options available constantly. Also, she was a twin and twins had always fascinated me.

Tori grabbed two more cherry tomatoes and placed them on top of her salad, making it look like a piece of art instead of something she was about to eat. It wasn't the first time I'd noticed she arranged her food in such a way.

"I like it," I said, nodding to it. "Edible art."

She smiled up at me. "Yeah."

We moved to pay, and then we made our way back to

our table. Tori sat next to me, and I tried to play it cool, but the entire right side of my body had sprung to life at the feel of her there.

"Dude." Walker shoved my shoulder. "You forgot to remind me to bring the cookies and deer jerky."

"Cookies and deer jerky?" Paris asked. "Where the hell did you get that?"

"Holt's mom. You've tasted her cookies before, but not her deer jerky. It's so good. The cookies too. The woman seriously needs to open up a shop. I'd keep her in business; that's for sure." Walker's eyes seemed to glaze over at the thought. The guy loved to eat. I'd picked up on that fact right away. Our first night at the academy, he'd raided the vending machines off every floor, stocking up on the things he liked most in case they ran out. It was something he did frequently. "I can't promise you'll get any of mine, but she's sending a package next month. I'll make sure you get something from it."

"Your mom sends packages for you? That's cute," Tori said before taking a bite of her salad.

I scratched my head. "Uh, yeah. I guess."

"I love how accepting she is of who you are now," Tori insisted. "That's great."

Were her parents not? I didn't know much about her other than she was recently bitten like the rest of us in our house.

"Yeah, both of my parents are pretty accepting. I mean, my dad doesn't understand certain aspects of it. He doesn't like to talk about it much either, but he accepts it. As best he can, I guess." I took a sip of my soda, hoping to wash away the bad taste lingering in my mouth. I didn't like talking about my dad. I wasn't sure why I'd mentioned him at all. Tori had a way of pulling things from me without even trying. "My mom, on the other hand, is just more suffocating now. Which is one of the main reasons I'm glad break is over. It feels good to be back here. To have a little space from her, as harsh as that might sound." I took a bite of pizza. The sensation I'd said too much bobbed in the pit of my stomach.

"I know all about the avoidance thing. My parents could give two shits about me now," Summer said. The sound of her voice startled me. I had forgotten she was there. All I'd been focused on was Tori. "I swear they're scared I'm going to hurt them. I'm glad to be back too. Can't wait till we can have a drink in our hands and can toast to that!"

I held my soda up as a wide smile spread across my face. "Cheers to that."

Tori set her fork down and shifted in her seat. Her eyes were on me. I could feel them, but it took me a minute to build up the courage to meet her stare. She was seeing me, but she wasn't. It was like her mind had dipped elsewhere.

"Maybe she's overcompensating for not being able to stop what happened to you. Like she's carrying guilt related to it. Parents are supposed to protect their children, and when they can't because of certain external forces, the guilt can sometimes tear them apart, forcing them to resort to being overprotective, overbearing, and a tad bit smothering." She licked her lips and blinked. Her eyes widened as though she couldn't believe the words had tumbled from her mouth, and averted her gaze from mine. "Maybe smothering you and baking cookies and stuff is just how she handles that guilt. I don't know." She tucked a few stray strands of baby hair behind her ear and resumed eating her salad.

"Wow. I've never thought of it that way," I admitted. "It makes sense."

It did. Mom had always wanted to protect me before, but after the attack, her desire to increased tenfold.

"Tori's good at all that psychoanalysis bullshit. Don't even get her started," Summer insisted.

"I'd say so." I was impressed.

This girl was beautiful and smart. She was the total package.

"Oh, hey." Paris perked up. "I just remembered there was a flyer for the next full moon run posted. I saw it on the way here. It's next week." She leaned back in her chair and exhaled a long sigh. "I don't know about you, but I'm ready. I didn't realize how much my wolf needs time in her fur and with a pack until I went home and was surrounded by my human family."

I knew my wolf well enough now to know that he didn't care about the pack mentality. He only cared about being able to run. That was what he yearned for.

"Next week seems like too long to wait," I said, without realizing it.

My wolf paced. He was as uneasy about the long wait as I was. When he snapped at me, I wasn't sure he'd be able to hold out for that long. He would need to shift sooner. It was against the rules to shift during unsanctioned times, though. And, that was one rule I had yet to break.

"It is," Walker insisted. He started going on about how it should be tonight or tomorrow night, but I tuned him out.

Tori had glanced at me. Her cheeks and neck shifted through at least four shades of pink before settling on one so deep it was almost red.

"I'm sorry about all that." She waved her hand around and flashed me a crooked grin. "Sometimes I get carried away. I end up pointing out things people don't want to hear about themselves. Sometimes, people they're close to too. Like what I said about your mom. It wasn't my place to analyze anything. Sorry."

"Don't worry about it. Really. I'm glad you said what you did. I've honestly never thought about it that way before."

A smile brightened her face, and I felt like I'd won the lottery. "Oh. Well. I'm glad I said what I said, then."

We fell into silence. I tried to shift my attention to what the others were talking about, but I didn't want the conversation to end between Tori and me so soon.

"So, um, how was your break?" I asked.

"Good. I enjoyed being home. It's nice to be back here, but I have to admit, I liked taking a break from it all." She wrinkled her nose and locked eyes with me. "It can be a little overwhelming sometimes."

"I know what you mean. Especially with the different houses."

"Exactly. It's taken me awhile to come to terms with there being hybrids of werewolves too. It's a lot to take in all at once on top of everything else."

I nodded. "Couldn't agree with you more."

"I mean, I'm fine with it now, though." Tori glanced around. It was clear from the look on her face she was worried someone from one of the other houses might have heard her. It was possible since we all had impeccable hearing, but one scan of those around let me know that no one was paying us any attention. They were all wrapped up in their own little worlds.

"We ready to head to Last Call?" Walker asked, drumming his hands on the tabletop.

Everyone seemed to agree, so we disposed of our trays and headed off campus.

THE WALK to Last Call was short. It took about twenty minutes, which was nice. I glanced around at the little shops as we walked. Brentwood reminded me of home. It had that small town charm going for it. The buildings looked like they had character and the sidewalks were decorated with planters of varying sizes.

When the sign for Last Call came into view, even my wolf seemed to sigh with relief. We were ready to let loose. Even though I wasn't the legal drinking age per the human government, I was in the supernatural world. It was one of the perks to becoming a werewolf. The tiny, but there nonetheless, silver lining I clung to.

Music played as we stepped inside the bar. The place was already slammed, but I knew it would be. Everyone was probably looking for a drink after making the trip from home back to the academy.

"Thank God it's not karaoke night. Some of these people really shouldn't step up to the mic," Walker said as we moved farther into the bar.

"Why? I think it's hilarious," Paris insisted. "The best performance I've seen was Finn Temple's rendition of Rod Stewart's *Do Ya Think I'm Sexy* last semester. He had this place going crazy."

"Correction: He had the women in this place going crazy because the dude couldn't keep his shirt on," Walker insisted.

"Very true." Paris grinned.

I glanced at Walker. Anger rippled off him. Not all of it was his. Most was his wolf's. He was a tad territorial when it came to Paris, and the thought of her being attracted to someone else rubbed him wrong. Walker had been working on it since they started dating.

The five of us stepped up to the bar, ready to order a drink. I offered to buy Tori and Summer's drinks, because I couldn't buy Tori something and leave Summer to fend for herself after Walker bought Paris's. I was a gentleman.

Even when I was broke.

"Holt," a guy muttered from beside me in a greeting. I glanced at him. The instant I realized who he was, I flashed him a wide smile and nodded hello.

"Axel. Have a good break?" I asked.

"It wasn't bad," he said before taking a swig from his beer.

His gaze drifted back to the dark-haired woman behind the bar. Faith was her name. I knew they were an item, so I didn't stare at her for long. Axel Stone wasn't someone you wanted to piss off. I'd seen him fight before. As a matter of fact, I'd gone against him in one. He was part of the underground fight club here at the academy, same as I was.

Axel was one badass dude.

And, not just because he was part of Wolf Blood and always tended to have that badass vibe coming off him like so many others from that house, but because of the way he fought. You got one swing, and if you hit him, you'd better pray you knocked his ass out because, if not, he would beat the crap out of you.

I knew from personal experience.

"Here you go," said Faith, Axel's girlfriend, and one of the few bartenders at Last Call, as she slid two beers and one mixed drink my way. "That's fourteen even."

I pulled out my wallet. Of course Summer's drink would be the one that cost seven bucks. Why had I expected anything less?

I flashed Faith a smile and handed her a twenty. Once I had my change, I said thanks and passed the girls their drinks before we followed Walker and Paris to a table near the back. My eyes drifted to Tori as I walked. Something was off with her. I'd noticed it before we left the dining hall. I couldn't figure out what had changed her mood, though I was certain something had.

TORI

I swallowed the first sip from my beer, hoping it would wash down my nerves. Why was I so worried about the sanctioned run that wasn't supposed to happen until next week? I should be focused on the drink in my hand, the music, and the company I was with like everyone else.

The problem was: I wasn't like everyone else.

Shifting into my wolf didn't excite me. It scared me. I couldn't control things while she was free like I could while human.

My wolf bristled at my thoughts, clearly not caring for them, and I downed another swig from my beer, hoping to sedate her. Did alcohol have that type of effect on her? I hadn't drunk enough since being turned to know. I tipped my bottle back again just in case. I was already upset with myself and my insecurities; I didn't need to feel her anger toward me about it all too.

"Dang, girl." Summer nudged me with her elbow.

"For someone who didn't want to come out tonight, you sure are enjoying yourself. I don't think I've ever seen you drink a beer so fast."

"Hey, no harm in that," Walker insisted. He lifted his beer in a toast. "We should all aim to enjoy ourselves a little more this semester."

Murmurs of agreement floated to my ears. I lifted my beer to toast with them, even though I wasn't feeling festive. I should aim to enjoy myself this semester, though. Maybe I should make a new list of rules with that being at the top. Or I could add it to my calendar as a reminder so it popped up every other Friday night. Better yet, I could block out that time on my calendar each Friday night and make sure it was a bright color so I'd notice it.

What was I thinking?

Normal people didn't make reminders for themselves when it came to having fun. They didn't pencil it in on their calendar either. They just did it. Without thinking. Without planning.

I took another long pull from my beer and hoped no one noticed how disgusted I was with myself.

"You okay?" Holt asked in a low voice as he tapped his beer to mine. I blinked, his question pulling me back to the moment. My gaze darted around. None of the others seemed to be paying attention to me anymore. Thank goodness. Paris and Summer had locked themselves in a conversation about shoes—which could last for hours—while Walker stared at Paris's boobs while sipping his beer, which could also last for hours.

"Yep. I'm fine." I flashed Holt a smile that I hoped was believable, and then swiped my bangs to the side. When I glanced at him, something in his eyes said he didn't believe me. "I'm just tired, I guess. There was a lot of family to see over the holiday. Most of them stayed with us too."

"Ah. Okay. I thought maybe something was bothering you." His green eyes narrowed.

Damn he was observant, even if he didn't realize it. How was it he could see me exactly as I was all the time? No one had been able to see me the way that he did. It made me uneasy.

"Nope. Nothing's bothering me." I lifted my beer to take another sip, but the look on his face made me pause. The ghost of a smirk twisted his lips, making him look sexy as hell. Mischievous even. "What?"

He leaned back in his chair. The sexy smirk that hung on his face never diminished. "Nothing."

A chuckle rumbled from deep within his chest.

"What's so funny, then?" I asked.

"Nothing is funny, per se. I guess I'm just calling bullshit is all."

I arched a brow. "And, what exactly are you calling bullshit on?"

Knots the size of my fist formed in my stomach as I continued to stare at him, hoping he hadn't been watching enough to realize the cause of my discomfort. If he mentioned the sanctioned run, I would be leaving. I didn't feel like getting into all the reasons why it freaked me out, and I damn sure didn't feel like listening to Summer lecture me on it again.

"Oh my God!" Summer shouted, causing my eyes to snap her way. I braced myself for her to dig in, thinking she'd been following our conversation, but she didn't. "I love this song!" she shouted before standing. Her eyes landed on me. I knew she wanted to dance, but I wasn't going anywhere.

I planned on sitting right here and waiting for Holt Taylor to explain himself to me. Summer shifted her gaze to Paris, having picked up on my mood shift. Paris jumped up almost as fast as Summer had and the two of them dragged Walker to the dance floor. The goofy grin on his face made it clear that he didn't mind.

Holt leaned his elbows against the table and stared at me. I could feel the heat of his eyes on my face. It caused my cheeks to grow warm. I hated that I blushed when I breathed.

"I'm calling bullshit on you for saying nothing is bothering you. I can tell something is. My wolf picked up on it. Your unease is lingering in the air around you. I can feel it."

He could feel my unease? I shifted in my seat, hating that he could sense anything about what I was feeling at all. He shouldn't be able to do that, should he? I could sense things with Summer sometimes, but I figured that was because I knew her so well. We were roommates.

Holt Taylor didn't know me.

"Well, yay for your wolf." I lifted my beer to take another

swig and was disappointed to learn there was barely a sip left. Wow. We'd been here less than thirty minutes. This was a personal record. Typically, I babysat my beers to the point of them being lukewarm because I wasn't much of a fan.

Clearly, that wasn't the case tonight. I came here with the hopes that the cure for my unease in regard to the sanctioned run rested at the bottom of my bottle.

At least a temporary one.

I was one beer in and still wasn't feeling it. I set my empty bottle down and leaned back in my chair. I folded my arms over my chest and refused to look at Holt, even though I could feel his eyes still on me. Instead, I found Summer and Paris living it up on the dance floor with Walker.

"Want to talk about it?" Holt asked.

"Nope." I kept my eyes on the others, watching as they had fun while the minimal amount of alcohol I had consumed flowed through my veins.

I barely ever drank, so a single beer was enough to have me feeling buzzed. It warmed me from the inside and had me bouncing my foot beneath the table to the beat of the song playing.

"Okay, then." Holt leaned in closer to me instead of away like I thought he would. I locked eyes with him when his knee brushed against mine beneath the table, sending sparks of electricity rushing through my lower stomach. Did he know he was touching me? "Can I buy you another beer?"

"Sure." My words were nearly lost in the bassline as a new song came on.

Holt downed the remainder of his beer before standing. He bent to grab my empty bottle and the scent of his sexy cologne invaded my nostrils.

God, he smelled good.

I sank my teeth into my bottom lip and forced my attention back to Summer and the others on the dance floor. Holt headed to the bar. Air filled my lungs again once he'd walked away. What was wrong with me? Why the hell did I let him affect me so much?

No, the question was: Why the hell did he affect me so much?

He shouldn't. I mean, he wasn't the first guy I'd ever had a crush on. However, he was the first I'd ever felt drawn to. What the heck was that all about anyway?

Summer waved her hands in the air wildly, catching my attention. When I glanced at her, she flashed me a wicked smile and then made an obscene gesture with her hand and mouth. Sometimes, she was as perverted as a guy. Still, I couldn't help but laugh.

"What's so funny?" Holt asked as he slipped into the chair beside me, and placed a freshly opened beer in front of me along with a shot of something.

"Nothing." My laughter died at his sudden close proximity and the abundance of alcohol he'd just set before me. "Just Summer's dance moves. She cracks me up."

"She does seem like a character," he said before motioning to the shots. "I bought us a little something more. You seem like you could use it."

I cocked my head to the side, eyeing him. "Do I?"

"Yeah." A grin spread across his face as he held my gaze. "You seem tense. Drink up." He reached for the shot glass in front of him, and I did the same.

I had no clue what the amber-colored liquid was, but I didn't care. All I wanted was for my mind to settle and my wolf to relax.

"On three," Holt said. "One, two, three."

He downed his shot at the same time I did mine. Our eyes remained locked, even as the liquid lava rushed down my throat to settle in my stomach. I winced, mouth hanging open, as I struggled not to inhale, knowing it would only flame the fire burning inside my mouth even more.

"Chase it with your beer," Holt insisted.

The amusement in his tone irked me. Still, I reached for my beer like it was a fire extinguisher and downed a few swigs. I panted, struggling to catch my breath after the fiasco.

"That. Was. Awful," I said between pants. "Yuck."

Holt laughed. It was rich, sexy, and contagious. Half a heartbeat later, I was laughing at myself right along with him.

"You're not a liquor person, are you?" he asked.

"Honestly, I'm not an alcohol person."

"I figured as much. I think I can count on one hand how many times I've seen you here."

I knew he meant well, but his words made me feel as though he was calling me out on not getting out much. I was sort of a shut-in. Always had been.

Awkward silence bloomed between us.

"So, um, are you excited about your classes this semester?" he asked in an obvious effort to keep the conversation going.

"You don't have to sit with me and chitchat," I said giving him a lopsided grin. "You can dance with someone if you want or whatever. I'll be fine."

He arched a brow. "Are you trying to make me go away?"

"No." Did that seem like what I was trying to do? My cheeks heated. "I'm just saying you don't have to sit with me and talk. Like, don't feel obligated to. I'll be fine."

"I don't feel obligated to sit with you. I like talking to you."

His honesty caught me off guard. I stared into his green eyes longer than I should, trying to see if he was being authentic in his admittance. It seemed as though he was. "And, why is that?"

The alcohol was making me bold. Brave. It caused the question that always came to mind whenever I was around Holt to bubble to the surface with too much ease.

Why was he interested in me? I needed to know.

Holt shrugged. "I just do. I think you're cool."

His lips pressed together the same way they had in the dining hall when he'd said I reminded him of his mom. When he wiped the palms of his hands on his jean-clad thighs, I knew the reason was because he was nervous.

Was he nervous because of me? Did I make him nervous? How was that even possible?

"Why don't the two of you quit yakking and get out

on the dance floor?" Walker shouted to us from over the music. His hands were cupped around his mouth when I glanced at him. "Let your bodies do the talkin' for once." A shit-eating grin spread across his face. Both Paris and Summer cackled like hyenas as they continued to move around him in perfect harmony.

A laugh erupted from me. I blamed the alcohol.

"And... I think the beers have gone to his head. Well, all of them really." Holt chuckled. "But, do you want to dance?"

"Sure. Let's go." The words scratched my throat on the way up, but I ignored the sensation and gave into the alcohol humming through my veins.

Holt's eyes widened. He hadn't expected me to say yes. Neither had I. I stood and held my hand out to him.

"Come on, before I change my mind," I shouted over the music.

Changing my mind would have been a good idea, because dancing with Holt Taylor definitely wasn't. Not with the alcohol flowing through my veins. Not with the way he smelled. And damn sure not with the way he looked at me as we walked to meet our friends.

A song with an upbeat tempo played, and I lost myself to the beat. My hips swayed. My hands lifted into the air, and my eyes closed as I moved.

Holt's hands fell to my hips. He invaded my senses with his closeness, and all I could think about was how much I wanted him. I spun around, positioning my back to him as we continued to move to the beat together. If I hadn't, I knew I would have kissed him. Summer danced her way toward me, sandwiching me between her and Holt.

"I'm glad you decided to let loose. You needed this!" she shouted over the music, her face lit with excitement.

"I did!" I agreed, the words rushing past my lips to disappear in the bass of the song playing.

A guy began bumping and grinding behind her, and she shifted her attention to him. I spun to face Holt. His teeth had sunk into his bottom lip, and his eyes were hooded with lust.

I could sense how much he wanted me in the air.

I licked my lips before moving to stand on the tips of my toes, and then I crushed my mouth against his. He didn't pull away. Instead, he moved his mouth against mine as though it were something we'd done a million times before. His fingers dug into my hips as I cupped the sides of his face, holding him right where I wanted him. His tongue snaked into my mouth to brush against mine, and I felt my knees buckle. I leaned into him, letting him become the only thing holding me up, and allowed my nerve endings to catch fire as our scorching kiss continued.

HOLT

I woke to my wolf irritated beyond belief. While it was true that I wasn't a morning person, it had become apparent my wolf wasn't either. Monday mornings seemed to be the worst for both of us. The only thing that motivated me to get out of bed was the chance that I might see Tori.

I hadn't been able to get her out of my mind. All I could think about was our kiss last night, which was probably why my wolf was so irritated this morning. Lack of sleep generally did that to him.

My feet hit the cool hardwood floor of the dorm room, and I let out a big yawn as I stretched. My gaze drifted to Walker. He was still in bed. His mouth was open and drool dribbled onto his pillow. I was about to chuck my pillow at him so he'd wake up, thinking he'd forgotten to set an alarm again, but it went off before I could. His cell buzzed to life with a weird ringtone that sounded like some crazy intergalactic music.

I grinned as I slipped out of bed and grabbed my slacks from on top of my dresser. They were clean-ish. I'd only worn them twice. While the clothes I'd taken home with me on break were clean, thanks to Mom washing them for me, my uniforms weren't. I needed to head to the campus laundry area at some point this week.

After I buttoned my slacks, I stepped to the closet for a white button-up. Cheeto bags from Walker littered the closet floor along with other trash and empty soda cans.

Jesus, Walker was a slob.

I pulled on my white shirt and then reached for the yellow striped tie Wolf Bittens wore. Usually wearing the tie didn't bother me, but this morning, I swore no matter what I did, it was too tight. My fingers fumbled to retie it again, but it didn't matter. My wolf growled, and I huffed a sigh of frustration.

I needed coffee. Lots of it. And, for Walker's alarm to shut the hell up. How had he not woken to turn it off yet?

I glared at him. He was still sprawled in bed as though he couldn't hear a damn thing. When someone in the dorm beside us beat on the wall, I knew I needed to cut the alarm off before the situation escalated.

"Hey," I said, shaking Walker after I'd shut his annoying alarm off. He didn't budge, so I shook him harder. "Wake up."

He mumbled something and swatted at me. I pulled in a deep breath and then tried again.

"Walker, I'm serious. Get your ass up." The words roared from me. Walker opened his eyes and stared at me like he didn't know who I was or what the hell was happening. "Get up. You're freaking alarm woke half the house. Why do you have the volume up so loud?"

I reached for my tie again, ready to give it another go.

"So I can hear it," Walker said. He sat up and rubbed the sleep from his eyes.

"Doesn't look like it does any good. I still had to be your mom this morning." As soon as the words fell from my mouth, I wished I could take them back. One thing I always tried to refrain from was saying anything about Walker's mom.

"I'm up. Jesus. What's your deal this morning?" he snapped as he swung his legs off the side of his bed while running a hand through his hair.

"I didn't sleep well, and I'm in desperate need of coffee because of it." I slipped my shoes on in a hurry.

"Really? I figured you'd sleep like a baby since you were practically lip-locking with Tori all night. Isn't that what you've always wanted?" A slow grin spread across his face.

"It is. It just... I don't know."

"I doubt she thinks it means y'all are a couple or whatever if that's what you're worried about." He stood and shuffled his feet to the closet. "You didn't marry her. You kissed her. Hell, maybe she'll regret it this morning. Who knows," he said, misinterpreting my awkwardness for the entirely wrong reason.

I didn't want her to regret our kiss. In fact, that thought hadn't even crossed my mind.

Shit. What if Walker was right? What if she did regret it this morning?

My chest tightened. It was easy to see how she might. Alcohol had been involved. And everyone knew that whenever it was, inhibitions were always set free. It was never a good thing.

Damn it.

I should've found a nice way to end the kiss she'd initiated instead of amplifying it. It should have been a simple kiss, probably like she'd intended it to be. I shouldn't have allowed it to turn into something as heated as it had.

I ran my fingers through my hair. Fuck, I might have screwed things up. What if she thought I'd taken advantage of the fact she'd been drinking? I had bought her a shot. Would she think my intentions had been to get her drunk so we could do more than kiss? No. She couldn't think that when she'd been the one to kiss me, could she?

My head swam.

The bottom line was it was just a kiss. We hadn't slept together. We might as well have for as much as our hands had been all over each other and as long as our lips had been fused together, though. If I knew Tori as well as I thought I did, she would be embarrassed about last night and probably really pissed at herself. Possibly even at me.

I grabbed my satchel, wallet, and ID card before heading for the door. I needed to fix this. I needed to smooth it over somehow. "See you later."

I left the room before Walker could reply. My feet moved fast as I headed down the hall for the guy's dorm and through the door to the staircase that led through the center of the house. I paused once there, and glanced through the mini-lounge, searching for Tori. She wasn't there. When a girl opened the door to the girl's hall, I glanced around her. Girls walked between rooms and their communal bathroom, but none of them were Tori. Had she already left the dorms this morning? Was she downstairs? Was she even in the building anymore?

I grabbed my cell and checked to see if she'd been active on any social apps yet. She hadn't, but that didn't mean she wasn't up. I'd learned in the short timespan I'd known her that she wasn't the type to stay on social media for hours. She didn't post often either.

Crap. Why didn't I have her cell number? It would make life a hell of a lot easier right about now.

I waited near the staircase for a few minutes longer before finally deciding to give up. It was a good thing too, because if Walker had seen me standing there, he'd never have let me live it down. He'd crack jokes about me being a lost puppy waiting on its owner or some shit. I didn't want to hear it. All I wanted was to find Tori and to make sure we were okay.

Once I made it out of the house, I booked it across campus to the student center so I could make it to the dining hall for coffee before first period. As I entered the building, Tori was the first person I saw. She sat at a table near the entrance with Summer and Paris. I stared at her, trying to gauge her mood, knowing it would be a good indicator as to how she felt about last night and us. She seemed fine. She smiled and laughed like usual as she picked at a muffin.

The tightness in my chest dissipated. Maybe I'd been overreacting. Maybe Tori was okay with what happened between us. Maybe it wouldn't be a big deal. Hell, maybe it would be the start of something amazing between us.

As I thought this, Tori's eyes locked with mine as though she could feel me staring at her. I flashed her a crooked grin. Her face paled, and my grin disappeared. I watched as her cheeks tinted pink before she averted her gaze, and I felt myself deflate.

Obviously, she wasn't as okay with what happened last night as I'd thought.

Summer glanced over her shoulder. When she spotted me, her lips twisted into a sad smile before she shifted her attention back to Tori. She said something that had Tori laughing, but neither of them looked back at me.

My wolf howled.

He was pissed and so was I. Although, I was positive we were pissed for different reasons. I was upset because I should have listened to my gut about the whole thing. I should've put the brakes on, and my wolf was pissed because my emotions were too much for him. He was already barely holding it together since I hadn't been able to shift. He hadn't had a release from all his pent-up energy surrounding the holidays yet.

Swallowing hard, I made my way to the line for the coffee machines. I didn't know what I needed to do to fix things with Tori, but the first place to start was probably to give her space. That had worked in the past with girls. If I gave them a day or two to calm down from whatever dickhead thing I'd done, then I could come to them with sympathy in my eyes and some smooth words to help gloss things over.

I wasn't sure those things would work with Tori, but I was down to try.

I stepped in line for the coffee bar behind a couple who couldn't keep their hands off each other and ground my teeth together. It wasn't a sight I cared to see. Not this morning. Not so up close and personal.

"Hey, man. What the fuck? You left the dorms like a bat out of hell," Walker said as he stalked to where I stood. His brows were pinched together and his face looked stern. The girl who stood in line behind me huffed. I cast a quick glance at her. She'd folded her arms over her chest as though she was pissed Walker had skipped ahead of her in line. I didn't blame her. Coffee was life. "What's going on?"

"I think I might have blown my one and only shot with Tori last night."

"Why do you say that? It looked like the two of you were hittin' it off fine."

He would think that. Hell, anyone who saw us would have thought the same. I knew better, though. Even so, I didn't have a clue as to how I could have gone about things better. Even if I'd tried to end the kiss she'd started before all the groping hands and moaning, she'd still be pissed at me today because she probably would have felt rejected.

It had been a damned if you do, damned if you don't situation. I'd been screwed either way.

"Well, I think she's regretting it this morning. She won't even look at me." I smoothed a hand over my face.

Walker glanced over his shoulder in Tori's direction. "Maybe she's just not a morning person, or maybe she didn't see you? Don't be so quick to judge." He slapped me on the back and then walked away.

The girl behind me let out a sigh of relief. I was sure it was because she was one person closer to that cup of caffeinated goodness she relied on to jumpstart her morning, same as I did.

Once I was finally able to get my coffee, I headed for the table where everyone sat, but the sight of Tori's stiff back had me second-guessing myself. I figured as soon as I stepped to the table she'd come up with some bogus excuse to leave so she wouldn't have to be around me.

To sit or to keep moving through the door? That was the question of the day.

I reached in my pocket for the quarter I kept there for tough decisions, setting my coffee on a nearby table. I ignored the people sitting there, wondering what I was doing, and balanced the quarter on my thumb. Heads, I walked to the table and sat down, pretending everything was peachy. Tails, I gave everyone a wave, said hello, and kept on walking through the double doors.

I pulled in a breath before flicking the quarter into the air. When I caught it, I covered it with my hand, exhaled, and then looked.

Tails. Thank God.

I grabbed my coffee from the table of strangers and slipped my quarter back into my pocket. My heart hammered as I wove my way through the dining hall toward everyone, but I never removed my eyes from Tori. As I grew closer, her posture became more rigid.

Was it because she could sense my nearness? Was that a good thing?

"Morning, everyone. I'll catch up with y'all later." I flashed a wide smile at everyone and made eye contact with them. Even Tori. I held my coffee up in a greeting and then kept on walking.

Tori was the only one who looked at me like I'd grown two heads. Had she been expecting me to sit so she could make an excuse to leave? Was walking away the right thing to do? Who knew, maybe my quarter toss had led me in the wrong direction and now I'd royally screwed things up with her.

That would be just my damn luck.

I headed outside into the cool morning air, gripping my coffee tighter than I probably should. Why the hell was I so bad at this with her? I'd never had an issue talking to girls or being around them before Tori.

This was all new territory. And, I was drowning.

My brows pulled together as I took a sip from my coffee. My wolf paced, his unease at my sudden rush of negative emotions getting the best of him. He had his own issues going on; he didn't need me adding to them. The sanctioned run was still six days away. I didn't know if he would be able to last without shifting. Hell, I didn't know if I would either.

My sanity was buckling.

I passed the basketball court, making my way to first

period. This semester it was Meditation and Spiritual Release. My eyes scanned the guys shooting hoops before class. Maybe that was what I needed. To play a game of ball to help blow off some steam? It had worked in the past. It was another thing last semester that had kept me sane while I waited between sanctioned runs and underground flights.

Speaking of underground fights, when was Bryant going to pass out invitations for the next one? He was the one in charge of the damn thing.

I scanned the court, but didn't see him. It was a longshot he'd be here so early. Even if he had, I didn't know that I'd say anything about fight club to him. It wasn't something we talked about. Mainly because it was against academy rules for the club to exist.

I took another sip from my coffee and sighed. Yep, today was going to be a shit day. That much was clear.

*H*olt just walked away from the table. He didn't even look at me for more than two seconds. Was he upset because I'd kissed him last night? Had I pushed things too far? He didn't seem to have a problem with it last night. After all, he'd been just as into the kiss as I was.

So, what was his deal?

He didn't have a reason to be nervous or embarrassed like I did. He hadn't initiated the kiss. I had. Besides, he was too good-looking to have those kind of self-conscious issues.

Right?

I hoisted my backpack higher on my shoulder as I maneuvered around a group of guys standing in the middle of the sidewalk.

"All right," Summer said from where she walked beside me. "Tell me what's going on in that pretty little head of yours. Did something I'm not aware of happen between you and Holt last night?"

"No. Why?" I risked a glance at her. Her attention was fixed on me.

"Then why are you two acting like you slept together and both regret the shit out of it this morning? Was he an awful kisser?"

"What? No. He was fine. And, we're not acting like that." I pushed my bangs out of my eyes. Why had I decided to get them in the first place? They were always in my way.

Summer positioned herself in front of me on the sidewalk and came to a standstill. She folded her arms over her chest and widened her eyes. It was the look she gave me when she was calling bullshit on whatever I'd said. My teeth sank into my bottom lip as I was reminded Holt had called bullshit on me last night too. I had a lot of people in my life who could see right through me.

I wasn't sure how I felt about that.

"Seriously? Is that how you're going to play this?" She tapped her foot on the sidewalk, her eyes never wavering from me. "I know something is up. I saw Holt walk in. He looked hopeful. Nervous, but hopeful. Until you blew him off."

"I didn't blow him off. He didn't even sit with us. He just got his coffee and left." My arms flailed when I talked. Why was I allowing this to get me so worked up?

"Maybe you should have smiled at him. Gave the guy some reassurance."

A long sigh pushed past my lips. "I'm being dramatic, I know. It's just, that was really out of character for me last night. I don't normally make out with guys at the bar."

"So, you're worried everyone is judging you because you made out with a guy at Last Call?" Summer started walking again. "It was Holt, not some random dude. I doubt anyone thought anything horrible about you. Heck, they probably saw it coming from a mile away like the rest of us. You two were destined to get together."

"You're right," I admitted. She glanced at me with a wide grin on her face. "I mean, about most of that. Not that last part. It was just Holt, not some stranger."

"Right. Even if it was a stranger, nobody cares. Everyone is so wrapped up in their own lives, I guarantee no one is paying as close attention to yours as you think." She took a sip from her coffee. "And, I mean that in the nicest way possible. That sounded really bitchy. Sorry."

"No, it's okay. I know what you mean." She wasn't being harsh or rude; she was being honest. Frankly, it was exactly what I needed to hear.

"Good." She linked her arm through mine as we continued walking. "Plus, it was just a kiss. It's not like you did anything else on the dance floor."

Exactly. It didn't mean we were dating. It didn't mean the kiss would lead to something more between us. Heck, it didn't mean it would ever happen again. A kiss was just a kiss. Nothing more. Nothing less. I'd been caught up in the moment, and apparently, so had he.

It didn't need to be a big deal. I didn't need to make it one either.

"Thanks, I don't know how I ever lived life without you," I said to Summer.

"There are many who feel that way about me." She winked and flashed me a grin. "Seriously, though. Why don't you give Holt a chance? He likes you. A lot. I can sense these things. He's a really good guy. If he was interested in me, I'd be all over that. Holt Taylor is hot."

My cheeks heated. He was. And, that was part of the problem. He was too hot. I didn't know how to handle being around him. I've never had a guy like him interested in me before. At least not that I knew.

"What was your first period class again?" Summer asked.

"Meditation and Spiritual Release." I didn't have to ask what hers was because I already knew—Essentials. I had both of our schedules memorized.

Plus, I'd had Essentials last semester. It was one of the classes at Lunar Academy that was segregated by house, which I didn't think was necessary. I understood why, but I thought it would be more interesting if they lumped us all together like other classes and let us learn about each of the houses instead of only our specific one.

"Right. Enjoy that." She took another sip from her iced coffee. "And, if you happen to see Holt again today, enjoy that as well." She winked before walking away.

"Ha. Funny," I deadpanned.

"Girl, I'm not even joking," she called over her shoulder. "Enjoy it."

I continued toward my Meditation and Spiritual Release class, knowing exactly where it was. I'd memorized the map given to us on the first day. Out of all the classes that we had to take at the academy, this was the one I thought of as the most pointless.

It had nothing to do with being a werewolf.

Then again, neither did Strength Training. A person didn't have to be strong to keep their wolf intact. Heck, they didn't have to be strong for them to shift with ease either. I thought of Strength Training as their version of P.E., and therefore, I hated it.

I stepped into the Meditation and Spiritual Release classroom, and the first thing I noticed was Professor Trinity.

"Hello, hello. I'm Professor Trinity. Welcome. Grab yourself a pillow from the bin at the back of the room and find yourself a spot in the circle." She motioned to the others forming a semicircle in the center of the room.

"Okay. Thanks," I said as I made my way farther into the room, heading for the bin.

I grabbed a pillow from the top—black with tiny white polka dots—and then started toward the center of the room to add myself to the circle. Holt was seated on one side of the circle.

I froze.

Why hadn't I felt him staring at me like I had every other time before? His eyes were on me. Had they been on me the entire time, or had he just now noticed me too? Either way, I swore excitement danced in the depths of his eyes, making their vibrant green seem even brighter. Was he glad we had a class together this semester?

Was I?

Where should I sit? Beside him? Beside the girl I knew from last semester, Cynthia? My heart beat out of control as I debated while standing there like an idiot. Also, how the hell was I supposed to sit on the floor in this skirt?

"Tori, hey. How was your break?" Cynthia asked once she spotted me.

I flashed her a smile and then stepped to where she sat. "It was good. How about yours?"

I could feel Holt's eyes on me. Was he pissed I hadn't sat next to him? Did it seem like a bitchy move?

"Eh, it was all right. Are you excited for this class?"

I shrugged, trying to ignore my inner turmoil as I situated myself on the pillow carefully. The last thing I wanted to do was flash anyone. "I guess."

"It seems like it'll be a piece of cake. I mean, how can we be graded on meditating? Or spiritual release? Those are both personal things. That's the only thing that's got me excited about the class—we're all guaranteed an easy A."

"I hadn't thought of it that way."

Holt's eyes were still on me. I could feel them. I tried not to pay attention to him, but even when I wasn't looking at him, my body focused on him.

"Okay, class, let's begin." Professor Trinity closed the door. She moved to the semicircle we'd created. I thought she was going to sit beside me, but instead so motioned for Holt and me to scoot closer. "The two of you move together. Let's close that gap up."

My heart leaped to my throat. I risked a glance at

Holt to judge his reaction, and he caught me. When his eyes locked with mine, I saw questions pooling in them. Maybe he wasn't being a jerk about the whole thing. Maybe he just didn't know how I was feeling and was trying to tread lightly.

Could that be possible?

He stood and grabbed his pillow before moving to sit beside me. The others did the same until the circle was whole. My palms began to sweat when he sat beside me. Inches were between us. Immediately, my thoughts dipped to last night. The way his hands had felt on my hips. The way his mouth had tasted. The way his tongue had slipped against mine.

My breath hitched. I was torturing myself.

"Looks like we're all here. I'll make my way around the room. When I come to you, I want you to tell me your name so I can put a name to a face," Professor Trinity said.

I groaned internally while my wolf paced. She was picking up on my emotions and didn't know what to do.

Once roll call was over, Professor Trinity did something I hadn't expected. She asked us to turn to the person beside us and tell them three interesting things about ourself.

I shifted to talk to Cynthia, but she'd already began chatting with the guy beside her. My throat tightened. Talking to Holt was my only other option. Fate was being hilarious today as she constantly pushed the two of us together.

What was I supposed to tell him? I couldn't think of

three interesting things about myself to save my life right now. Still, I had to try.

"Hey," I said, not knowing how else to start a conversation with him. Especially after everything.

"Hey, yourself." An easy smile spread across his face. My wolf settled, and so did my erratic heart.

I licked my lips and dropped my gaze to the floor. I could do this. "So, we have to tell each other three things about ourselves."

"Ladies first."

My lips pursed together. Always a gentleman. I'd hoped he would have taken the lead on this so I could copy his questions. "Well. Hmm." My teeth sank into my bottom lip. I couldn't think of a single thing he might want to know about me, let alone one to get the ball rolling. "Three things. Let's see."

"It doesn't have to be anything crazy," he said to reassure me.

It actually took some of the pressure off. "Right. Okay, I had a perfect GPA my senior year in high school. My favorite color is teal. And, I like lemon-flavored things." A satisfied smile twisted my lips as I brushed my bangs from my eyes.

There. That was easy enough. At least I thought it was. Until I looked at Holt.

He stared at me as though he was waiting for me to continue. No, that wasn't it. He seemed unimpressed with my three things. Heat crept up my neck.

"Were those not good enough?" I asked, being serious.

"Eh, they were okay. I just already know them. I was hoping to learn three new things about you."

I searched his face for any sign that he was joking, but didn't find one. "What do you mean you already know them?"

How was that possible? I was positive I'd never told him my GPA in high school. Maybe he would be able to guess my favorite color, but I didn't think I'd ever told him that either. And, I knew I'd for sure never mentioned lemon being my favorite flavor.

Holt shifted on his navy blue pillow, and ran a hand along his jawline. The scratchy sound of his fingers against his stubble had me wanting to rub my fingertips against it. There was something about a guy with five o'clock shadow that did things to me.

"They're obvious. Everyone knows you're smart, so you having a perfect GPA in high school isn't any surprise. Hell, you probably have a perfect GPA here. Right now. As for teal being your favorite color, anyone who isn't colorblind can guess that. Your nails are always teal. Your wallet is teal. And, so is your backpack." He flashed me a cocky grin.

"Okay, well I bet you didn't know about my love for all things lemon," I countered.

His grin grew. "You always seem to have an endless supply of lemon candies on hand."

I didn't know what to say. He'd been watching me. Close. Part of me was excited by this new knowledge.

"I'm guessing you want me to say three more things

about myself, then. Ones you wouldn't know. Right?" I asked while secretly hoping he said no.

"Absolutely."

My stomach dropped. Crap. Now, I had to think of three more things to tell him. My worry was in vain because immediately three more things came to mind—how much I liked him, how much I wanted to kiss him again, and how being close to him had my heart feeling like it was about to pound out of my chest. None of those passed my lips, though.

"I love photography. Nature scenes are my favorite. And, I miss my dog." I looked at him, hoping to see some sort of acceptance of my answers flash through his eyes, but all I saw again was his desire for me to say more.

"That's two. You still owe me one more," he said.

I shook my head. "That was three. Photography. Nature scenes. My dog." I ticked each off my fingers as I spoke.

"Oh, sorry." He chuckled. "I thought your love of photography and nature scenes were one thing."

"I forgive you," I teased. "Your turn. Tell me three things about you." I tried not to sound eager to hear what he had to say, but I really was.

"All right, three things about me." He licked his lips, drawing my attention to his mouth. Immediately, I was tossed back to the memory of last night and how they'd felt pressed against mine. "I love good barbecue. The works. Pulled pork. Barbecue chicken. Ribs. Brisket. I could eat it nearly every day. Fishing is one of my favorite pastimes. Bass fishing. Trout fishing. Both are fun. I've never much liked fly fishing, though. And, for my final thing, I guess I'll say that I have a tattoo and a piercing."

I arched a brow. That last one wasn't something I'd been expecting. However, it was the one that had me the most excited.

I gave him a once-over, searching for his tattoos but mostly for his piercing. "I'm not seeing any piercing. Is it in a crazy place?"

Did he have his nipples pierced or was he into freaky stuff and had something lower pierced? Hadn't my hands been all over his solid chest last night? I tried to think back to if I'd felt anything suspicious beneath the cotton of his shirt.

"No crazy place. There's not an earring in it, so you probably can't even tell it's there." His fingers lifted to smooth over his brow. "Technically, it was only pierced for about forty-eight hours before my coach noticed and made me take it out. There's scar tissue there if you touch it just right."

I wanted to touch it. I wanted to touch him. But I refrained.

"Cool," I said, hoping I sounded nonchalant and not as fascinated as I was. It was fun trying to imagine what he had looked like with his brow pierced. I bet it had made him look even sexier.

Not that he needed it.

"As for the tattoos, I guess it's really considered two pieces, but they form one."

My interest piqued. "Can I see?"

Holt glanced around the room. Was he making sure

everyone was focused on their own conversations, or was he checking to see where Professor Trinity was because his tattoo was in a bad place? I sort of hoped it was in a bad place. My cheeks heated at the thought.

When Holt untucked his shirt and lifted it to reveal his muscular chest, my face caught fire.

Dear lord, he had a nice body.

"What do you think? Normally, people have questions about what it means or why I chose it," Holt said, pulling me back to the moment.

I blinked once, and then averted my eyes from his amazing body to the tattoo inked across his skin. It was unlike anything I'd ever seen.

A beautiful wolf took up his entire left pec. Its mouth was open wide, and its sharp fangs dripped with saliva as it bit down on a skull. The skull was detailed to the point of nearly looking 3-D. The shadows and shades of its hollow eyes were impressive, but it was the open mouth, releasing a silent scream that drew me in. Pain. Agony. Sadness. I felt it all was reflected in his tattoo.

My throat pinched tight.

"It's... um... wow." I was at a loss for words. Never had I seen anything like it. "What does it symbolize?"

I shifted my gaze to lock with his, knowing a person didn't get a tattoo of this caliber without it meaning something to them. It wasn't like getting a Chinese symbol you thought meant mystery when you were drunk and out with some friends.

This was different.

Holt released the edge of his shirt, covering his tattoo again. "Maybe one day I'll tell you," he said with a wink.

Professor Trinity spoke again, and I remembered we were in class. My attention shifted back to her, but for the remainder of class, all I could think about was Holt—his tattoo, his abs, and his lips.

When class was over, we headed to the back of the room where the bin was and tossed our pillows inside.

"I showed you my art," Holt whispered as he leaned closer to me than necessary to toss his pillow into the bin. "Now, how about you show me yours?"

"I don't have any tattoos," I said before I could think through what he was asking.

He laughed. "I'm talking about your photography."

My heart kick-started. "Oh, right."

I rarely showed anyone my photographs. They were for me. No one else.

"What time tonight works for you?" he asked. "I mean, are you free?"

"Tonight? Um." My mind blanked as I struggled to remember if I had anything I needed to do. Was this a date? Or was it truly about seeing my art? Tattoos were art. I knew that. But this felt like maybe it was something more. "Anytime, I guess."

"How about seven? I can come over then."

"Come over? To my dorm?"

"Yeah. Unless you have your pictures on your phone." He ran a hand through his dirty blond hair, his green eyes never wavering from mine.

"Oh. Right." I squeezed my eyes shut. "No. All the

good ones are on my laptop. I'll have to weed through them."

Panic clawed its way up my throat. I wasn't ready to show him anything yet. I needed to find the right files. There were a few I had in mind.

"So, does seven work for you, then?" he asked.

"Could we move it to seven tomorrow night?" I hated to ask, but knew I needed time to prepare. Something flashed through his eyes, but it disappeared before I could label it.

"Okay, yeah. Sure." Holt smiled. "Seven tomorrow night. Works for me."

"Great." My mouth grew dry.

Holy hell. I'd just agreed to hang out with Holt Taylor tomorrow night and show him my art. Summer was going to lose her freaking mind.

HOLT

$\mathcal{I}$ thought I'd been clever in asking Tori to show me her art since I'd shown her mine. I wasn't exactly sure where the idea or words had come from, but I was glad they found their way to me, nonetheless. However, I was disappointed when she'd said she would rather meet up tomorrow night at seven.

Beggars couldn't be choosers, though.

I swiped my ID card—which was also used as our form of currency—in the vending machine and punched the buttons for the bag of chips I had my eye on. Next, I got myself something sweet. I'd made it through the first day of classes this semester unscathed and felt like cele-brating. I could've saved myself money and celebrated by eating a few of the cookies Mom sent me home with, but I'd had so many already that I was sick of them.

"Hey, Holt," Teddy, one of the first guys I met at Lunar Academy besides Walker, said as he stepped in line behind me for the vending machine. "It's cool we have a class together this semester. Although, Professor Blades sounds intense."

Professor Blades was the teacher of the Strength Training class they offered here at the academy. He had to be from the Wolf Blood house, though I couldn't be sure. All the teachers here seemed to either wear a black tie or they didn't wear a tie at all. Professor Blades was one who decided to forgo the tie.

"Definitely." I nodded.

"I'm thinking he's Wolf Blood," Teddy said as he rocked on his heels. "What do you think?"

"Same." I stepped out of his way so he could get to the machine. "They all seem to have that same level of intensity."

Except for one. Lee Twain was the only member of the Wolf Blood house I thought of as a nerd. The dude had a serious comic book obsession. And, even during fight club, he was an awkward character. Intense wasn't a word I'd use to describe him.

"I think it'll be a good class, though. I'm down for burning off some of this pent-up energy. I still haven't gotten used to it." Teddy scratched his head. A look crossed his face that I could relate to—it signified he felt overwhelmed.

"I know what you mean." I slapped him on the back. "I'm sure it will get better, though. There has to be a point where everything on the inside balances out."

It was the first time I'd said the words out loud, but it wasn't the first time I'd thought them. I knew there was some truth to them because I'd seen it. Within myself.

Balance was obtainable. You just had to break—or bend, depending on how you looked at things—the rules a bit. Fight club was how I did that. And, so was Tori. Being around her seemed to ease my mind and my wolf all at once.

I started to walk away, but Teddy spoke again.

"How much do you think Professor Blades can bench press?"

It was a topic shift, but I didn't mind.

I stepped to the soda machine and swiped my card. Mom would have a fit if she saw me loading up on so much junk food. She was all about homemade meals with simple ingredients. Processed foods were the devil in our house.

I'd missed out on so much growing up, but I was healthier for it so there was that.

"I'm not sure, but I'm willing to bet whatever it is, it's way more than I can." I chuckled.

"Right? The dude is seriously ripped. I'd pay to see someone go against him in a fight."

I nodded. "Oh, yeah."

My mind filled with faces from fight club. All of them were students, but I was positive there were a few teachers and staff members everyone would love to see on the roster. Professor Blades was one of them, but I couldn't imagine who'd want to go against him. If I had to pick someone, I'd pick Bryant, though. The guy was as ripped as Blades and just as intense.

Now that would be a fight I'd pay money to see.

I didn't mention a word about it to Teddy though. He

wasn't part of fight club, which meant he wasn't allowed to know about it.

"I'll see you later." I popped my soda open, took a swig, and started for the stairs.

I held my snacks tight and my soda tighter as I jogged up them. If I couldn't shift, or fight, or be around Tori tonight, I had to do something to settle my wolf. When I didn't focus on something—anything—I felt myself slipping into that huge sea of depression I struggled daily to avoid. Cardio was something to focus on. It was something to help settle not only my mind, but also my wolf. Professor Blades mentioned the same during Strength Training earlier today. He'd said it was how he kept his two sides from warring with each other.

It was in that moment I became grateful I was Wolf Bitten and not Wolf Blood. With all the inner turmoil I had going on already thanks to my wolf, I knew I wouldn't be able to survive if a vampire had been tossed in there, too.

I'd almost made it to my dorm when something besides my snacks appeared in my right hand. Excitement pump through me. I knew what it was without having to look.

An invitation... to fight club.

I set my drink and snacks down in front of the dorm door and unfolded the scrap of paper that had magically appeared in my palm. I had no clue if there was a timer attached to it, but I remembered from previous invitations that it would disintegrate soon, leaving behind only the faintest hint of magic across my fingertips.

Midnight. The woods. Everyone fights.

My wolf howled out his excitement as a wicked smile twisted the corners of my lips. This was exactly what I'd been waiting for—a way to release some pent-up energy and keep myself in check.

The paper started to disintegrate. In two seconds flat, it had completely disappeared. All that remained was the faint scent of magic and a tingle of heat tickling my hand.

I brushed my palm across my slacks and then bent to retrieve my soda and snacks from the floor. A wide grin plastered to my face. I whipped out my ID card and entered the dorm. Walker was unbuttoning his uniform shirt when I stepped into the room.

"Holy crap, got the munchies?" He eyed my snacks.

I chuckled, my mood inexplicably happy. "Yup."

Walker's brows pinched. "What's up with you? You're too happy. It's freaking me out."

I laughed and shook my head as I set my things on the desk we shared, and then kicked off my shoes. "Am I not allowed to be in a good mood?"

"Not this good of a mood. Unless..." His brows lifted to his hairline.

"Unless what?" I opened my bag of chips and shoved a few in my mouth before loosening my tie.

A smirk twisted across Walker's face. "Unless you managed to get some action during your first day of classes. Tori kiss you again? Maybe give you a little something else?"

"Fuck off." I threw a chip at him.

He held his hands up as though surrendering. "I'm just sayin' that I've never seen you this happy. It can only mean one thing."

"Whatever, dude." I rolled my eyes. Still, my grin wouldn't die down.

"Okay, so you didn't get any sexual favors. And, she didn't kiss you. That can only leave one thing."

"What would that be?" I asked, humoring him.

"You asked her out, and she said yes."

Damn, he was good.

He wasn't that good, though. My good mood wasn't solely because of Tori and the somewhat date we had tomorrow night. It was also due to fight club happening at midnight.

"You did, didn't you?" Walker pressed.

"Yeah, I did. Tomorrow night. Seven o'clock. I'm supposed to meet her at her dorm."

"Bow-chicka-wow-wow," Walker said as he made this obscene gesture of smacking someone's ass while he danced around the dorm.

Sometimes, the guy was a total tool. Even so, I still loved him.

* * *

I waited until five minutes till midnight before I left the dorms and headed to the woods for fight club. Walker wasn't back yet. He'd met Paris earlier, and I imagined the two were doing exactly what he'd insinuated Tori and I should be earlier today. Most nights, I hated when he came in late, but tonight it had worked out perfectly, considering I had someplace else to be and would rather not have to explain where.

I said hey to a few people in the small lounge area as I made my way to the stairs. While it was true there were curfews in place, the house was never locked down. I'd learned that early last semester. We were allowed to come and go as we pleased. The only curfew-related rule I'd seen enforced was the one about there being no members of the opposite sex in dorm rooms past midnight. However, like Walker, there were a few who didn't abide by this rule.

As I walked, no one stopped me to ask where I was going or what I was doing out so late. When I made it outside, the cold night air felt good against my heated skin. After a few steps, I passed the faculty and staff building without anyone saying a word, and then I was almost to the woods. The closer I came, the more intense the feeling of eyes being on me became. I wasn't alone, but I was okay with that. It was probably Bryant, watching as all of the members made their way to the first fight of the new semester.

I inhaled a deep breath. Damn, it felt good to be out here.

I slipped into the woods and my wolf paced with anticipation. Partly because he was ready to run. To give into his fur and pound his paws against the damp earth as he pushed himself through the night. He also was eager to see me go head-to-head with someone again. There was a level of pleasure he took in seeing me beat some-one's ass.

The half-mile trek into the woods felt like it took forever, but I knew it was a trick of the mind. Both my wolf and I were excited to be here. Excited for a fight. When I finally stepped into a clearing, I relaxed. And, so did my wolf.

Bryant wasn't standing among the others, but I knew he would be soon. I nodded to everyone. Some shook my hand. Some slapped me on the back. Here, there were no houses dividing us; there was only an ability to fight and a certain level of respect that came with it.

As soon as Bryant came into the clearing, he made his way to the center of the group.

"Evening, everyone. I hope you've all had a good break. Same as I hope everyone here is ready to fight. I'm sure you've all got some pent-up energy, same as me. How about we get that energy out?" His eyes scanned over each of our faces. "Pair up. I don't care how. Biggest man against smallest. Girl against guy. Hell, I don't care if it's against someone you've already fought before. Find yourself a challenger. Now."

Electricity hummed through my veins as I scanned those around me. Who did I want to go against? Who wanted to go against me? My gaze paused on Axel Stone.

"Down for a rematch?" he asked, popping his knuckles as the curve of a smile twisted his mouth.

I stepped forward. "Absolutely."

"Everyone have a challenger?" Bryant asked.

"No. Not everyone. I don't have someone to go

against," someone said. When his voice cracked, I looked to see who the poor sap was.

It was Lee Twain.

He was dressed in one of his stupid comic character t-shirts and looked like he was about to hyperventilate. What was he so scared of? His last fight he'd creamed the guy. One punch was all it had taken. Granted, the guy was smaller than Lee, but still. He'd taken him down and seemed to have gained a hell of a lot of confidence because of it.

Where was that confidence now?

"Guess you're with me, Twain," Bryant said.

My stomach bottomed out. Immediately, I felt awful for Lee. No one wanted to go against Bryant. Not even me. He was one scary looking guy. The only person I'd say who might revel in the thought of going against him was standing across from me. Axel Stone. He could take Bryant easily.

His roommate, though? Not a chance.

Lee blinked. "Uh, are you serious?"

"Deadly," Bryant insisted.

Lee swallowed hard. "Okay."

I grinned at him. Maybe he had bigger balls than I'd given him credit for.

"Okay," Bryant said with a smirk. "When I count to three, I'm gonna push this button on my phone and everyone can begin fighting. The fights stop when one of you taps out, passes out, or the bell rings."

I glanced at Lee. His face looked a little pale. I was positive it was because he knew he was about to get beat.

I directed my attention back to Axel. My feet shifted apart, placing myself in a fighting stance as I continued to hold his stare. I'd learned a lot since the last time we'd gone toe-to-toe, and I was more than ready to show him.

A slow smile formed on Axel's face. He was just as ready as I was for this.

We all were.

"Fight!" Bryant shouted.

I lunged forward, sending the first punch soaring through the air. It connected with Axel's jaw. It barely rattled him, but I felt like it had nearly broken my hand. He was solid muscle. When he chuckled, I knew I was about to get my ass handed to me. He swung and missed. I'd felt the air off it; he'd been so close. My adrenaline spiked, and we began our dance of the night.

TORI

I paced the length of my dorm while I waited on Holt to come. I'd been waiting for this moment all day, but now my stomach decided to twist into knots the size of my fist. Summer had left thirty minutes ago to meet a guy from her Essentials class for drinks at Last Call, which meant there was no one around to talk me out of my panic.

My gaze fell to my watch. Ten minutes. He would be here in ten tiny minutes. My throat pinched tight. The desire to look through the photos I'd picked out for him to see shifted through me again. I resisted. It had taken me hours to dig through everything. Nothing had seemed perfect enough. I wanted to showcase my best work, the stuff that anyone would find beauty in, even if it was marginal, but it had been hard. I was too indecisive. Too critical of my own work. I imagined that was how every artist was, though.

We all knew exactly how to tear apart something we'd found beautiful while creating.

My gaze skimmed the pictures I'd laid on my bed. Since nature scenes were my favorite, and I'd been told they were a strength of mine, I decided to go with the few reels I'd had developed of the woods surrounding the academy. I'd also tossed in a few shots of the campus at sunset and sunrise. Now that I was looking at them, they seemed pretentious. Maybe Holt wouldn't think so. Maybe he would focus on the sky being lit with all the vibrant colors behind the backdrop of the Gothic buildings. Still, my heart pounded. Showing anyone my photographs always had me feeling as though I were standing in front of them naked while they inspected every inch of my body.

My teeth sank into my bottom lip as I glanced at my watch again. Seven minutes.

My mind circled what I would say to introduce Holt to each picture. I played through different responses I thought he might give, and then tried to imagine where the night would go afterward. A person could only look at pictures for so long. I hadn't pulled up many. Fifty maybe, but I didn't think he'd actually get through them all.

I imagined he would make it through the first twenty before becoming bored.

A knock at my door startled me. I glanced at my watch. Five minutes. If it was Holt, he was early.

My mouth grew dry as I stepped to the door. I pulled

in a deep breath, trying to steady myself, and fixed my expression into one I hoped came off as warm and inviting instead of nervous to the point of puking.

"Hey, you're early," I said as I swung the door open, coming face-to-face with Holt. He was dressed in a pair of jeans, a green plaid shirt that made his eye color brighten, and a pair of shoes that looked like ones a person would wear on a hike. There was a slight bruise under one of his eyes and a cut on the side of his chin.

Had he been playing basketball again?

I knew he played with a few of the guys from our house sometimes. They were a rough bunch. At least, I thought they were, given the cuts and bruises that always seemed to appear on his beautiful face after a game with them.

Holt ran a hand through his dirty blond hair. The expression on his face looked boyish and cute. Immediately, my nerves relaxed, and my attention on the remnants of his latest basketball game escapade faded to the back of my mind. "Yeah. I know. I couldn't hold out any longer. I've been pacing the hall for a good fifteen minutes now, maybe longer, trying to decide when I should knock on your door."

"If it makes you feel any better, I've been pacing the length of my dorm for a while too. I wouldn't have minded if you'd come earlier."

He grinned. "If only I'd trusted my gut and knocked when I first thought, neither of us would've wasted so much time suffering."

I stared into his eyes, loving what he'd said more than I should. "If only."

Why did he have to be so cute? Why did I have to fall for him so hopelessly fast? And, why did I second-guess myself constantly for it? I wished I could be more like Summer. She always let loose and waited to see where the moments took her. Not me. I was a damn stick-in-the-mud.

"Are you planning on inviting me in? Or did you want to go someplace else? The dining hall or out for coffee maybe?" Holt crammed his hands into the front pockets of his jeans, his eyes never wavering from mine.

My hand slammed against my forehead. I stepped to the side. "Oh. Shoot. Yeah. Come on in. Sorry." My face flushed through twenty shades of red. I could feel it. My cheeks were on fire. "I pulled everything up on my laptop, and set out a few prints. Nothing fancy. They're just a few pictures I thought were decent."

My heart pounded as he stepped into the room, closing the door behind him. Holt walked to my bed where the pictures were laid out, keeping his hands in his pockets. I exhaled the breath I hadn't realized I'd been holding and stepped to his side. I tried to remember the things I'd planned to say once he was looking at my pictures, but my mind was a blank void. All I could think about was him being in my room. Inches away from me... from my bed. His eyes were on my art, soaking in pieces of my soul. His opinion mattered more than I thought it would, and I waited for him to say something.

Anything.

"These are fantastic," he finally said, but I couldn't tell if he truly meant it. I couldn't see his face because I was too much of a coward to lift my eyes and look. All I wanted to do was hide. Why had I agreed to this? "The way you've angled the camera to capture the full length of the academy and get so much of the sunrise behind it is breathtaking."

Air filled my lungs. He liked it. I could hear it in his tone. Well, my wolf could.

"Thanks." I moved to clasp my hands behind my back. If I didn't, I'd reach out and touch him. He was too close, and with such a limited amount of space between us, it was hard for me to think.

"I love this one too." He pointed to a photo I'd taken before winter break. It was of the woods behind the faculty and staff building. "The way the fog is rolling in. The clear sky above. The little dots of stars barely visible. And, those shadows where the trees stand. It's haunting in the best of ways."

My mouth dried up. That was exactly what I'd been thinking the moment I snapped the image. Holt understood art. He understood me.

That thought scared the shit out of me.

I licked my lips. "Uh, yeah. The contrast I was able to capture at the moment was definitely haunting. That's what I was thinking when I took the picture."

Holt shifted to stare at me. "Is this all you planned on showing me, or is there more?"

There was a hungry look in his eyes that excited me.

It made me want to show him more. To bring him further into the world behind the lens with me.

"I have more pulled up on my laptop if you want to look at them. I wasn't sure if my pictures would be your cup of tea. All art is very person specific as far as their tastes." I stepped to where my laptop sat open on the desk and tapped the mouse pad, bringing the computer to life.

His eyes were on me. I could feel them. Heat crept up my neck, reddening my skin.

"I want to see as much as you're willing to show me, Tori." My name coming from his lips was everything. "You're really talented. I mean that."

"Thank you." I pushed my bangs out of my eyes, and motioned to my laptop. When his attention drifted from me to the screen, I pulled in a breath. "These are from sort of all over. It's an accumulation of a few of my favorites I've taken throughout the years." I moved aside so he could sit at the desk and view the images at his own pace.

Minutes ticked by without him saying a word. I said a few things here and there in regard to each of the pictures that he seemed to pause on for longer than the others, trying to explain my motivation behind taking them or what I was attempting to capture. His silence made my stomach twist.

Maybe he didn't think these ones were as good as the others. He was a hard person to read.

"Do you have a favorite?" Holt surprised me by asking once he'd reached the final image in the folder. "Not of the ones you showed me, but of all-time." His eyes lifted to lock with mine, and it was clear he genuinely wanted to know.

"I do." I bent at the waist to pull up the image on my laptop. The movement placed us closer to one another, causing my entire left side to tingle and pulse with his nearness. My wolf panted. I knew it was because she wanted him as much as I did. My teeth sank into my bottom lip, hoping he couldn't sense her desire or my own. "This one."

I shifted back to standing, allowing him space so he could see the image for himself. It didn't matter if he liked it or not, because it was my favorite. There were so many emotions attached to the memory of when I'd snapped the image that no words anyone ever said about it would be able to tarnish it for me. It would always be my favorite.

"Holy shit. I love it," he said. "Wow. The way they're looking at each other as they enter the woods. The dusky night sky as the backdrop behind them. I love everything about this picture."

I folded my arms over my chest and shifted on my feet. "Thanks. Me too. The wolves in it are actually my parents."

"Your parents are wolves?"

He shifted to face me. While we might have known each other since the beginning of school, we didn't know every detail about one another. We each had our own stories about how we came to be what we are, and I guessed this was the moment where I told mine.

I wondered how Holt would react when he learned

I'd went into this wolf thing willingly. There seemed to be so many in Wolf Bitten who wouldn't have chosen this life for themselves had they been given the choice. I wondered if Holt would be one of them. While I didn't know the story of how he'd come to be what he was, I figured there was probably anger attached to it because he often seemed pissed about things.

I flashed him a small smile and shrugged. "Yeah, they are."

"How are you Wolf Bitten if your parents are wolves? Wouldn't you be Wolf Born instead?" His confusion was palpable. I understood why.

"Um, well yes. Technically. If they were my biological parents, but they're not. I'm adopted."

Holt's eyes widened. "Oh. Sorry. I didn't know."

"It's nothing to be sorry about. And, you're right, you didn't know. Not many do. It's not something I like to talk about. Summer knows, of course, but no one else. Not because it bothers me, but because it doesn't matter. My parents are my parents. They raised me. They're the only parents I've ever known."

"How old were you when you were adopted?" he asked and then licked his lips. "I mean, you don't have to answer that question if you don't want to."

"Four. I was with them for almost two years before that though. As their foster kid. They weren't able to have kids of their own for whatever reason, so they decided to foster. I was the first foster kid given to them. Thankfully, they said they fell in love with me quickly and wanted to keep me. They filed for adoption as soon as they could." Warmth centered in my chest as I remembered the story.

"That's amazing. I'm glad you had a good childhood and found a happy home with them, but how is it you became Wolf Bitten?" The question burned through his eyes.

"I found out what they were." My gaze dipped to my laptop. "Actually, the night that picture was taken was when I found out they were werewolves."

"How old were you when that happened?"

"Eight."

His eyes bugged. "You were only eight-years-old, and yet you thought to take a picture of them in wolf form instead of running out of the house screaming?"

"What can I say, I've always loved photography. Especially when it comes to nature." I chuckled. "It helped that they were always good to me too. I knew in my gut there was no reason to fear them. Not even while they were in their wolf form."

Holt ran his fingers through his hair. His Adam's apple bobbed when he swallowed hard. "Did you choose this life?"

"Yeah, I did." I nodded, but continued to hold his stare. It felt important. I'd gathered the sense that he was trying to see if I was lying, and I needed him to know I wasn't. "I love them. They had already brought me into their family. They accepted me. And, by choosing this, I accepted them. Fully. I have no regrets."

The look that shifted over his face had me thinking he would never have chosen this life for himself had he been given the choice. Our paths were different, but we still ended up at the same place. Lunar Academy.

It was funny how life turned out that way sometimes.

"Would you have chosen differently?" I asked, knowing the tension in the room wasn't going away until he'd said his piece.

His jaw moved back-and-forth as his eyes grew glossy. I wondered where his mind went. Had he gone back to the moment he was bitten? Or was he somewhere else?

"My story isn't as happy as yours," he said after another few seconds ticked away. "This wasn't something I chose for myself. It was something forced upon me out of anger and blind rage."

His hands balled into fists as they rested against his thighs. He shifted to sit back in my desk chair, and I could feel his anger rippling off him in waves. My wolf paced as my teeth sank into my bottom lip. I wanted to say something to him, but I didn't know what. No words would come. Maybe it was for the best, because I knew there was nothing I could say that would change his past. And, it was clear that changing his past was the only thing that would make him feel any better about what happened.

"I don't like talking about it much. All I'll say is that you asked earlier what my tattoo meant." He lifted his gaze to lock with mine. His eyes burned with the same intensity his words held. All the air in my lungs pushed free, and my mouth grew dry as I held his stare. "The wolf is symbolic of my wolf. The skull is symbolic of me. Of who I used to be. When I was bitten and became this, it killed me. It killed my dreams. My hopes. It killed everything I ever was from before that moment. It broke me. That tattoo is a reminder of how my wolf and that moment ate me away."

I couldn't breathe. I couldn't look away from him. My knees grew weak as they struggled to keep me upright as emotions rushed through me from his honesty. I could sense his heartbreak, his anger, the revulsion he felt when he thought of who he was now. It all pulsed in the air around him, filling my dorm room and suffocating us both.

I stepped closer to him without realizing I had and sank to the floor beside him. I placed my hand over one of his closed fists. His breath hitched and then I heard it push past his lips as the rigid muscles of his body relaxed.

"Becoming a wolf didn't break you. It bent you when it forced you in a new direction. That's all." The words came easily. They pushed their way past my lips as though speaking them would breathe life into Holt. "Life does that to everyone."

Holt didn't speak. Instead, he leaned forward and kissed me.

His lips pressed against mine, sending my heart rate spiking. I hadn't expected him to kiss me, but I was more than okay with it. My wolf seemed to be too. Without much thought, I moved from where I crouched beside him to his lap. The heat radiating off his body moved through my thin leggings, scorching my skin. His mouth continued to work over mine as his fingers dug into my hips. I sucked his bottom lip between my teeth, nibbling just a little.

I lost myself in the moment. Thoughts of how he tasted even better than I remembered floated through my head, followed by the realization that I was definitely falling hard and fast for him.

HOLT

The first couple of weeks back for the semester went by fast. However, I was coping better than ever. Fight club had resumed. I had one sanctioned run behind me. And it seemed as though Tori was always at my side. We hadn't made things official yet, but to me, we'd been official from the very first kiss.

Tonight, I was going to make sure she was on the same level as me.

I was nervous, even though I shouldn't be. I could tell Tori was into me. Sexually and intellectually. It was something my wolf was able to pick up on easier than I could. He'd sensed it in her. I'd chalked it up as one of the perks that came with having him.

"Now, dig deep with your heel, squat, and lean slightly forward as you extend your arm. Do this in one fluid, rapid movement. Strike," Professor Blades instructed, pulling me from my thoughts of Tori and tonight. "And, strike," he shouted again, signaling we do the same move for a second time.

My core burned. My legs wobbled beneath me. Sweat dripped from my eyes, but I still continued. I still put in an effort to do as many as he asked and to push myself hard.

When would he end the torture though?

We'd been going at it for nearly thirty minutes now, and there didn't seem to be an end in sight. Professor Blades had been exactly the type of professor I thought he was—intense, strict, and determined to whip our sorry asses into shape by the end of the semester.

"And, release," Professor Blades said, causing a sigh of relief to trickle through the entire class as we all shifted out of the lunge position he'd had us locked in for far too long. "That will be all for today. I'll see you Monday." He gave us a nod and then clasped his hands behind his back before he walked to his office without another word.

I'd grown used to his coldness. He rarely said to have a good weekend, or have a nice night. He only said what was necessary and not a word more. I sort of respected him because of it.

"Please tell me your calves are burning as bad as mine right now," Teddy said as he hobbled close to me.

"I might not even be able to walk out of here," I huffed.

Teddy twisted the top off his water and took a long swig. "I know. I like how toned I'm getting, but damn. Dude is like a drill sergeant."

"I know what you mean."

I grabbed my water bottle off the floor and twisted the cap off to take a swig. The cold water felt amazing against my dry throat. However, I was so overheated I felt as though the water were boiling before it reached my stomach.

"Me and a few guys were planning on heading to Last Call tonight, if you want to come along. We'll probably head out about eight or so," Teddy offered after he took another swig from his water.

I wiped the sweat from my brow with the edge of my tank and flashed him a lopsided grin. "I would, but I have plans with Tori."

Teddy lifted his brows. "Ah, so the two of you are an item. I've been wondering. I've seen you two together more often than not lately."

My grin grew. "Yeah, I think it's safe to say we're definitely an item."

"Good for you," he said as he patted me on the back. "I'm happy for you, man. You know, she's welcome to come to Last Call too. Some of the other guys will probably have their girlfriends with them. Tori is a cool chick. I like her."

He started toward the double doors and I followed him. I was eager to step outside. It was like a damn oven inside the Strength Training room. I had no idea how Professor Blades stayed in there so many hours out of the day. You would think the place was heated during the winter months, but it didn't seem as though it was.

Not that it mattered. By the end of class it was like a damn sauna from all of us breathing so hard.

"Thanks, will see. We might," I said as I started toward the Wolf Bitten dormitory. Teddy was by my side until someone from class called him back.

"I'll see you later. I mean, if you two decide to swing by Last Call. If not, have a good weekend, bro. I got to go talk to Rich for a second," Teddy said before he jogged away.

I glanced at Rich. He was from Wolf Bound and we had Strength Training together. I didn't know much else about the guy besides that.

What did Teddy need to talk to him about?

My cell chimed with a new text. I pulled it out of the drawstring bag I always took with me to Strength Training and glanced at the screen. It was from Tori.

Hey. Was just thinking about what you asked me this morning. Froyo. Cheesecake.

I smiled as I reread her message while I walked.

I think that can be arranged. Can't wait to see you tonight.

I hesitated before I hit send because I wasn't sure if I should erase that last part. In the end, I decided to leave it because it was true. Every time Tori wasn't with me, I couldn't wait to see her again. It was a strange sensation. One I hadn't ever felt before her.

Good. And, I can't wait to see you tonight either.

A lightness centered in my chest at her feeling the same. I tossed my phone back into my drawstring bag and slung it over my shoulder. Sweat trickled down my forehead. After I wiped it off, I twisted the cap off my water bottle and took another swig. I was ready to head to the dorms and shower in preparation for tonight. We were going out for dinner and then dessert. I'd asked her earlier what her favorite dessert was. Froyo was her answer. Even though I wasn't much of a fan—I preferred ice cream—I'd gladly eat froyo if it meant I was able to spend time with her.

* * *

"Man, I wish I was going out with you tonight instead of staying here," Walker muttered from where he sat in our desk chair, sulking like a two-year-old. "I can't believe Paris is making me stay in tonight."

I chuckled. "It's for a good reason, though."

He rolled his eyes, and I laughed.

Paris had said the two of them needed to stay in and work on their first assignment for Moon Phases that was due on Monday morning. Both of them had been notorious for procrastinating until the last minute to do any projects or assignments last semester; Paris decided that wasn't how she was going to be this semester. She'd decided that neither was Walker. Instead of waiting until the night before, she felt they should give themselves two full days to get the project done. While I still wouldn't have been comfortable cutting it so close, it was a slight improvement from how they handled things previously.

"Yeah, yeah." Walker pouted. "I would've got it done on time. So would she. What does it matter if we do it the night before or two nights before? I tried to explain this to her, but she doesn't understand."

I slipped on my shoes and then reached for my jacket. "I think the whole point is that she wants you two to do better this semester. That means getting things done sooner than you were last semester. When you have more time to do something, you're able to make a better product. I think that's what she's getting at."

"Still doesn't make a damn bit of sense to me," Walker insisted.

"I don't know, dude, but I need to head out. I don't want to be late meeting Tori," I said. We'd agreed on meeting at 7:30, so by the time we walked from the academy to the only Mexican restaurant in Brentwood, Nachos, it would be close to eight and the dinner crowd would hopefully have cleared out so we could have speedy service and snag a good table. "I'll talk to you later. Leave a sock on the door handle or something if you and Paris plan to knock boots. I don't want to walk in on something again."

Three nights ago, I'd walked in on them doing the deed. While I wasn't squeamish when it came to nudity, the two of them together wasn't something I cared to see again anytime soon.

"Noted." Walker flashed me a wicked grin.

His mind had clearly dipped to thoughts of having a repeat of the other night instead of doing his assignment. I had no doubt that was probably how the night would end regardless of whether the assignment was finished the way Paris intended.

I left our dorm and headed down the boy's hall. When I pushed through the doorway separating our hall from the lounge area, Tori was waiting near the stairs. She wore a pair of dark skinny jeans, a lavender sweater that contrasted well against the blue of her eyes, and her signature scuffed up Converse. Her hair was pulled up into a high bun on top of her head, and her slender neck was visible. She looked incredible. My mouth grew dry. I crammed my hands into the front pockets of my jeans, adjusted myself, and tried to will all the blood heading south to pause in its descent.

"Hey, there," I said when I stepped to her. I licked my lips and cleared my throat. She flashed me a smile that looked sexy as hell. "Are you ready to eat?"

"I'm starved." She placed a hand on her stomach.

I motioned to the stairs. "After you," I said with the intention of sounding like a gentleman. Really, all I wanted was for her to go first so I could check out her ass in those jeans. I was going to hell for sure. She glanced over her shoulder at me as she started down the steps and caught me. I coughed into my hand. It didn't hide what I'd been doing. "So, um, what else do you want to do this weekend?"

"I was thinking of going on a hike. I did a little research and noticed there are a few trails around here. I mean, I guess it's to be expected since we're in the mountains, but still." She rolled her eyes and grew animated as she talked.

When a group passed us on the stairs, I fell into step beside her.

"Want any company on your hike? I can't remember the last time I went on one. It would be fun."

Hiking was the one thing my parents enjoyed together when I was growing up. Well, until Dad blew out his knee at work one day and it never healed right. It became his bad knee overnight and fishing became his new hobby. I'd taken to fishing quickly as well. Mom had been disappointed for a while—hiking had been her favorite—but she'd found herself a new hobby pretty quick like Dad had.

Baking.

"Do you even like to hike?" Tori asked as she paused on the landing for the second floor lounge for another group to pass. Once they did, she waited until I was beside her again before continuing down the final two flights of stairs to the main level of the dormitory. "You don't seem like the hiking type. Actually, when you told me you were into fishing, I almost didn't believe you."

"What? Why?" I chuckled.

"I don't know." She shrugged. "You just don't strike me as the type who likes to hang out outside unless it's something sports related. I get jock vibes from you. Not nature lover."

Her assessment of me would have been right this time last year. "Yeah, well... that's not who I am anymore, regardless of the vibes I send out."

Silence built between the two of us. I knew I was being a real Debbie Downer, but I couldn't help it. Her words were a reminder of who I'd used to be, who I wasn't anymore.

I'd known then who I was and what I wanted out of life—a quarterback who was about to be given a full scholarship to a university and planned on being a coach because he loved the sport that much.

Now, I wasn't sure who the hell I was anymore or what my future held. I was lost.

"Do you want to talk about it?" Tori asked when we finally pushed our way through the exit of the Wolf Bitten dormitory and stepped into the chilly night air.

I ran a hand through my hair and refused to meet her gaze. Her eyes were on me, I could feel them, but I could also smell her sympathy in the air as well as her confusion. My wolf paced. He didn't like the nosedive my emotions had taken. It had put him on edge.

"Not really." It was an honest answer, even if it wasn't the one she'd been hoping for.

"Okay, no problem. I totally understand. So, back to the hike," she said, surprising me with how at ease she was with me refusing to let my walls down. It was nice. It made me want to kiss her even more. "I'd love some company, if you're willing to come with me still. There were about five or six close hikes to this area, but I picked one with a waterfall and a meadow because I haven't photographed either in a while. The app I'm using says it's an easy hike in the shape of a loop and that it isn't very long."

"Not very long, huh? Doesn't seem specific."

She chuckled, and I was glad because it meant the mood had been shifted to something less dramatic and awkward. "It said it was like 2.4 miles long, but that it was easy."

"Those apps tend to lie. You do know that, right?" I teased.

"I'm down for trusting it. It doesn't matter to me how long I'm out there, as long as I have some water, a few snacks, and my camera. If you aren't up for that hike, there was another one that's about a mile long. It's a paved road instead of an actual trail through the woods, but it's supposed to have a beautiful scenic view at the top." She glanced at me as she spoke, and I could tell a hike was something she was looking forward to. "It has a cool name too—Devil's Courthouse."

"Woo. Sounds spooky," I said as we continued walking off campus and toward downtown Brentwood where Nachos was located. "And, it's been a good while since I've seen a waterfall. How about we do both? We could do one Saturday and one on Sunday?"

We paused at a crosswalk. I pushed the button so the little walking man would change from red to white quicker. At least I thought that was what it did. Maybe it didn't. Maybe the button only gave people the impression that pushing it did something when in actuality the duration of time a person stood there waiting for the little man to change colors was the same regardless.

"Sounds good. Time spent outdoors is definitely something I need lately," Tori insisted.

"The sanctioned run a while back wasn't enough for you?" I teased.

I was positive everyone at the academy would agree

with me when I said there weren't enough sanctioned runs. In fact, there shouldn't even be a rule when it came to shifting. We should be allowed to shift at will. With or without a pack. As long as we stayed on the academy grounds.

Something in Tori's demeanor shifted, capturing my attention. I couldn't pinpoint what it was exactly, but I knew that her happy-go-lucky attitude had disappeared. It had to have been because of something I'd said. Was she having a hard time dealing with the limited number of sanctioned runs we were given? Or was it something more?

"I was just joking." I tossed my hands up in mock surrender. My lips twisted into a smile, but it didn't do me any good because Tori didn't glance at me to see it.

"I know. I just... I'm not big on sanctioned runs. Or shifting. Like at all." Her eyes never left the sidewalk. My wolf picked up on the anxiety rippling off her, and I knew she was serious.

"You don't like to shift?" I couldn't hide my surprise. How did she not like to shift? That was one of the few good things that came with becoming a wolf. I'd never felt freer than when my wolf was running wild.

While I knew there were some who thought of this entire thing as being a curse, Tori wasn't one of them. She couldn't be—I mean, she'd chosen this for herself.

So, why did shifting freak her out so much? She knew it was part of the package.

"Not really." She lifted her gaze to mine. The light on the crosswalk turned, and we started to move across the street. "It's not that I don't like my wolf; it's just that she's a little more carefree than I'm used to being."

"What do you mean?" I didn't understand what she was trying to say. How was her wolf more carefree than she was used to?

"She's not easy to control. She relies a lot on her instincts, which isn't something I'm used to."

I scratched my head. "I'm still not following you. Relying on your instinct is a good thing. And her not being easy to control is probably because she's an animal. I think maybe that part takes time."

"Yeah, I know." She licked her lips. "I'm just so used to being in control of all aspects of my life, and this is one where, when I allow her to take over and I set her free, I can't control her the way that I want. Not really. And, that scares me."

Her words made her sound so vulnerable and the way her shoulders drooped forward made her seem small. Fragile.

I grabbed her wrist, bringing her to a standstill in the middle of the sidewalk with me, and pivoted her so she was facing me. I lifted her chin, forcing her eyes up to meet mine, and then I said, "It's okay to be afraid. Every single one of us was at some point or another after being bitten. I'm pretty sure it's normal. Same as I'm pretty sure you're exactly where you need to be to learn to not fear your wolf. So kudos to you for finding your way here and for toughing it out with the rest of us because it's not easy some days. I know that better than most. Please, just stop thinking you're weak or not in control, or whatever, because I don't see you that way. You're smart, beautiful, brave, and strong."

Without saying another word, I kissed her.

It was supposed to be a sweet, peck on the lips, but when she leaned into me and intertwined her fingers in the hair at the nape of my neck before snaking her tongue out to brush against my bottom lip, the kiss went to another place.

Time seemed to tick away slowly... until an asshole in the tiny silver car decided to honk his horn at us as he passed. When we pulled apart, we were both out of breath, and I swore there was nothing in this world that could dim my smirk.

"That was amazing," I said, still out of breath.

Tori shook her head. "No, that wasn't amazing, you're amazing. Thanks for not making me feel stupid for admitting this whole wolf thing sort of freaks me out even though I said it was something I wanted."

"You don't have to thank me."

"I feel like I do. You were supportive about it, and you made me feel better about something that's bothered me for a while."

"Have you not told your parents how you feel?"

Her eyes widened. "No. I can't." She untangled herself from me and crammed her hands into the back pockets of her jeans before continuing to walk toward Nachos. "It would crush them. They already have enough regret about what they did. I can see it in their eyes. I don't want to make them feel bad about something I told them I wanted. They tried to talk me out of it, but I swore I'd thought about it and that it was what I wanted. I honestly thought I'd be okay with it. I thought my wolf and I would have this amazing connection. What I didn't expect was to feel as though something foreign had been placed inside me I couldn't get rid of. That's awful, I know. My wolf deserves someone better than me."

"I'm sure that's frustrating, and while I don't necessarily feel the same way about my wolf, I do understand how this whole thing shook you up. Trust me, I get it."

Tori glanced at me. "Thanks. For listening. For not criticizing me. For being you. It felt good to finally talk about it all with someone. Even though I'm sure my wolf hated it—she's pacing."

"Cut her some slack, Shewolf. Tori is doing the best she can," I said as I leaned in, hoping her wolf heard me.

Tori laughed, and there was no better sound. Ever.

I held the door open for her and we stepped inside Nachos. The scent of spicy food and cheese dip lingering in the air, making my mouth water, but it was Tori's laughter that had a smile stretched across my face. Tonight was turning out fantastic.

*A*fter we ate at Nachos, we headed to the coffee shop, which also served Froyo. I opted for mixing cheesecake and strawberry together while topping it with salted dark chocolate chunks. It was like heaven in my mouth.

Holt had mixed together all of the frozen yogurt options available, creating a cheesecake, strawberry, chocolate, peppermint combo that I didn't think tasted half bad.

"That's good. I actually wish I'd thought of it," I said as I licked my spoon clean.

"I told you it would be good. And don't worry, we'll come back sometime soon so you can get your own." He winked. I loved it when he winked at me. It was sexy, and always sent butterflies fluttering through my stomach.

"You were right." I took another bite of my froyo before speaking again. "I just can't believe you didn't put any toppings on it. I mean, who forgoes toppings? They're the best part."

"I think I have enough flavor punch happening without added toppings." He laughed.

"True."

As we continued down the sidewalk, headed back to the academy, my gaze drifted to Last Call across the street. Music flowed from inside as a group of girls stepped outside for a cigarette. People stood around outside the doors, smoking cigarettes and chatting. It was a little after nine and the place seemed packed.

"Want to pop in and grab something to drink? I don't think beer or liquor pairs well with froyo, but I'm down for it if that's where you want to go," Holt said as he caught my eyes positioned toward Last Call.

"No, I'm fine. Beer and liquor definitely don't mix with froyo."

"I don't know," he teased. "We might be able to make a crazy float mixing the two together."

"Yuck!" I wrinkled my nose. Eating a strawberry cheesecake beer float with salted dark chocolate chunks sounded disgusting. I opened my mouth to say exactly that, but a commotion taking place in front of Last Call captured my attention. Holt glanced that way too. "Isn't that Teddy? From our house?"

"Yeah."

We both watched as Teddy shoved another guy farther from the entrance to Last Call. He stumbled, but attempted to head back inside despite Teddy's clear warning against it.

"Who is that with him?" I asked, eyeing the other guy. He was short in stature, but buff. I'd seen him before, but he wasn't from our house. "He's in Bound, isn't he?"

"Yeah. His name's Rich," Holt said. "He's in my Strength Training class."

Rich got in Teddy's face, and while Teddy didn't seem like the fighting type, he had his back to me, leaving me unable to gauge his expression.

"I should go see if everything's okay. It looks like Teddy's having a hell of a time rounding up Rich," Holt said. He glanced at me with sympathy in his eyes. I knew it was because he didn't want to end our date or detour it down this path—neither did I—but whatever was going on between Teddy and Rich looked serious. "Are you okay with that?"

I nodded. "Absolutely. Let's go see what's going on."

Holt wasted no time placing his hand against the small of my back and steering me across the street in their direction. I ate another spoonful of froyo before tossing the cup and spoon in a trash can we passed.

When we reached the two, I had no idea what was going on, but my wolf was able to feel the situation out quickly.

Shifter magic was in the air.

"Shit," Holt muttered a millisecond later. "This isn't good. We need to get Rich out of here."

My gaze locked on Rich. Shifter magic oozed from him. He was about to release his wolf. Right here in front of everyone.

"I know," I said.

While it wouldn't be horrible if he did, it wouldn't be good either. Brentwood was a supernatural friendly town, but that didn't mean there weren't humans among its residents who were oblivious to the supernatural world.

"Rich, come on, don't do this," Teddy pleaded. There was a faint slur to his words, and I knew I was right in suspecting both of them had had a few drinks tonight. "You don't want to do this, man."

Rich shook his head. "It's time."

"No. Listen to him, buddy," Holt insisted. He stepped closer and leaned in. "Keep your wolf in check. It's better for everyone if you do," he whispered.

I focused on Rich. He seemed distraught, pissed, but distraught. What had set him off? What made him think shifting in front of all these people was okay? That it was something he needed to do?

Was he spelled?

Rich was in Wolf Bound. Even though they weren't allowed to use magic outside of the classroom or on their own, that didn't mean everyone in Bound followed that rule. I'd witnessed a few from that house use magic before. Once, I was pretty sure a girl used magic to get rid of a hickey on her neck in the bathroom of the student center building. I hadn't blamed her, but still. Bounds used magic in ways that broke the rules sometimes.

Was this one of those times? Had someone spelled Rich to reveal his wolf to these people so he'd get in trouble with the academy?

"Those assholes deserve to know they're not better

than me. They aren't better than you. Or you. Or you," Rich slurred as he pointed to each of us standing around him. "They aren't shit compared to any of us. And, I'm going to show them why."

Okay, so the theory of him being spelled by someone in his house as a prank or out of anger was knocked off the table. Apparently, he was just pissed at some jerks inside the bar.

"Who is he talking about?" Holt asked Teddy.

Teddy ran his fingers through his hair. "Some group of guys inside who are complete jerks. They've been heckling just about everyone for the last hour."

"Yeah, because they're fucking assholes who need to be put in their place," Rich insisted through gritted teeth.

His eyes flared as more shifter magic rolled off him. He reached for the collar of his shirt, and in one swift movement, tore it from his body. The fabric split down the center as though he'd taken a pair of invisible scissors to it, revealing his toned chest and abs. The veins in his neck bulged as he let out a growl that was more animal than human.

"Let me go back in there and show them who the hell they're dealin' with," Rich shouted. Spit flew from his mouth when he spoke.

I took a step back, not because of the spit, but because of how scary and intense he was behaving. Rich was dead set on showing those fools who they were messing with. I didn't know if anything we said would be able to stop him. He seemed to have reached beyond the point of reining in his wolf.

"Chill," Holt insisted. He reached for Rich's arm. "Those guys aren't worth the trouble you'd get yourself in with the academy and then some."

He was right. Who knew what kind of trouble Rich would find himself in if he went through with this.

"Why don't we go for a walk," I suggested, thinking it sounded like a good idea.

"Holt is right, man. They aren't worth getting expelled, or worse," Teddy insisted, piggybacking off what Holt said and seeming to ignore my suggestion of going for a walk.

His odd wording did give me pause, though. What would be worse than being expelled from the academy? I couldn't think of a single thing besides being killed, but the academy wouldn't do that to Rich for revealing his wolf to humans.

Would they?

I focused on Teddy. He seemed even more uneasy than the situation called for. Sweat beaded along his brow as though the stress of the situation was making his heart pound. Did he have anxiety? I didn't know him well enough to answer that question, but from the times I'd ran into him in the Bitten house, I didn't think he suffered from it any more than the next person.

His eyes shifted to look at those surrounding us. A small group had formed. People were curious about what was taking place. A fight. An argument. And then there were a couple who seemed to be watching Rich heavily. Had they overheard enough to know what Rich wanted to do?

"Let's go back to the academy," Teddy insisted as he locked eyes with Rich. "Before the E—" Teddy glanced around again. He swallowed hard and then returned his gaze to Rich. What had he been about to say? And who in the crowd had made him think twice about saying it? "Before you do something stupid. This isn't the time or place for that and you know it."

Chill bumps swept across my skin because there seemed to be a double meaning in Teddy's words. He'd accentuated certain words too much. Hadn't he? Or was I making a big deal out of nothing? Maybe I was picking apart the situation more than I should.

Just when I thought the situation had been defused at Teddy's last words, Rich started swinging. Holt barely missed taking a punch to the jaw. Teddy wasn't so lucky. Rich busted him in the nose, sending a spray of blood down the front of his shirt. My hands covered my mouth as a gasp slipped free.

Holy crap!

I took another step back, giving the guys distance to scuffle with one another. Words obviously weren't going to defuse this situation. Action needed to be taken.

"Dude, I'm telling you right now, you don't want to fight me. Trust me on this," Holt insisted as he ducked another blow from Rich. I was impressed with his reflexes. However, I knew he had to have gained some fast reflexes over the last few weeks since I was seeing fewer marks on him from the basketball games he played. I still didn't know when he found the time for basketball, but somehow he did.

Teddy shoved Rich, and a group of girls standing close by smoking a cigarette squealed. Their heels clicked across the concrete of the sidewalk at a rapid pace as they moved back.

"What the fuck, Rich?" Teddy shouted. Blood continued to drip from his nose, but he didn't seem to care. He was focused on Rich. "I'm trying to help you. I'm trying to keep you from doing something stupid. Don't you understand that?"

Holt reared back and sucker punched Rich while he was distracted by Teddy. The hit was so strong, Rich stumbled, falling to the ground. His lips twisted into a smirk and a chuckle bubbled from his throat. He reminded me of a cartoon character who'd been hit with something and was seeing stars.

"Sorry, but you left me no choice," Holt said. A shaky breath pushed past his lips, and I knew it was because he hadn't wanted to hit Rich. "You left me no choice."

The shifter magic clinging to the air dissipated.

"Doesn't matter," Rich said. He spit a bloody lougee on the sidewalk with his eyes still locked on Holt. "You can stop me today, but it doesn't matter because you're not going to be able to stop the revelation. It's coming. Regardless." Rich passed out before he could say another word.

I had no idea what he was talking about, and one look at Holt made me think he didn't either. Teddy clearly did, though. His expression said it all.

"We should get him out of here," Teddy insisted. He

stepped to pick Rich up. "Before the cops are called or something."

Holt moved to grab hold of Rich's other arm. "Yeah. What was he talking about, though? What revelation is coming?"

"He's drunk," Teddy insisted. "I wouldn't think too much on what he says. He's not making sense. Just help me get him back to the academy, back to his dorm."

Holt's eyes shifted to mine. We both knew Teddy was lying. He was hiding something. Something Rich had been ready to reveal.

"Should I call a cab or an Uber or something?" I asked. "Walking back to the academy carrying him seems a little excessive." I pulled my cell from my back pocket.

"I can take you," someone said from behind me. "We can all pile into my SUV."

I spun to see who it was and came face-to-face with a guy I'd seen around the academy. He was a Bound, if I remembered right, and his name was Lionel.

"Are you sure?" Holt asked.

"Yeah, absolutely." Lionel retrieved his keys from his pocket and motioned for us to follow. He was headed toward a black SUV parked a few spaces away.

The guys followed, hauling Rich along with them. I hung back a few steps, taking in the expressions of those around us. A few people seemed to stare for obvious reasons, but there was one guy with a scar who seemed to stare a little too heavily. A shiver slipped up my spine. I didn't know who he was, but it was clear from one look he was from Wolf Blood, which meant he was part vampire.

What had Teddy, and Rich for that matter, gotten themselves into?

Lionel popped the back door of his SUV open so Holt and Teddy could shove Rich inside. The two of them sandwiched him in the middle, and I situated myself in the front with Lionel. A purple cardigan caught my eye. It had to belong to his girlfriend. I'd seen him around campus with a girl before. What was her name? It started with a G, that much I could remember. She was always studying, and there were rumors about her not holding any magic earlier in the year. I wondered if things had worked out for her.

Lionel placed his keys in the ignition and cranked the engine on his SUV to life. "So, what happened?" Lionel asked as he backed out of his parking space. There was a slight smile that twisted his lips. "Did Rich get hammered and start a fight?"

"Yeah," Teddy answered before any of us could. A look of suspicion dulled Lionel's features. I knew it was because of Teddy's quick response.

"Sounds about right," Lionel insisted as he headed toward the academy. "He's a good guy, but he likes to raise hell."

That much was clear.

I leaned back in my seat and shifted to look out the passenger window. It was about a ten-minute drive from downtown Brentwood to the academy, but it felt like an eternity. Awkward silence filled the vehicle that didn't break until Rich began to rouse.

My chest tightened. I hoped he wouldn't start swinging. Relief trickled through me when he didn't. Instead, Rich cupped the side of his face.

"Ouch. Damn. What happened?" Rich muttered without removing his hand from his jaw.

"Apparently, you were running your mouth a little too much. Again," Lionel said with a chuckle as he turned into the academy's garage. He found a parking space and cut the engine on his SUV. "Thankfully, these guys were able to get you out of there before you caused any trouble."

I swallowed hard, wondering how much Lionel had seen. Had he come from inside Last Call to ask us if we wanted a ride, or had he been coming from somewhere else and conveniently been parked close to where we were? I hadn't paid enough attention to know the answer to either question.

"I need something to drink," Rich said with a moan.

Teddy opened his door and slipped out. "Yeah, I don't think you need anything else to drink tonight."

"Water. I meant I need some water. And something to eat. And apparently a new shirt." His fingers played with the scraps of what used to be his shirt.

"Let's get you to the Wolf Bound dormitory. I'll buy you something from the vending machine," Lionel said as he slipped out of the driver seat.

"You sure you've got him on your own?" Holt asked. "I don't mind helping get him inside."

Lionel waved Holt's words away. "I'm good. He's up and walking now. So, at least that's an improvement over how he was when you guys shoved him in my backseat."

Lionel was a good guy. I liked him.

"All right, well thanks for the ride. Have a good night. I'm sure we'll see you around," Holt said. He placed his hand against my lower back and gave Lionel a small wave.

"You too. And thanks again for taking care of this guy," Lionel said as he nudged Rich with his elbow in the ribs.

"Dude, don't even," Rich muttered. "I feel like I'm gonna barf."

"Thanks for your help." Teddy started toward the exit of the garage. It was clear he was trying to get away from us. Probably because he knew we wanted to grill him about what happened and why he'd lied.

"What was that all about back there?" I asked as I followed him. "You didn't answer our questions."

Holt was at my side in an instant. It was odd how I didn't even have to look to know he was there; I could feel him. When had that happened?

"I think there's some explaining that needs to happen," Holt said when Teddy remained mute.

Teddy crammed his hands into the front pockets of his jeans as he counted toward the Wolf Bitten dorms. "Not really."

"Why was he rambling on about a revelation coming? Is he religious?" Holt pressed.

"If that's what you want to believe, sure." Teddy picked up his pace.

"Um, we want the truth. Not some bogus lie." My words were harsh, but I was sick of the back-and-forth already.

Teddy paused outside the doors to our dormitory. He shifted to face us, his eyes skimming over us both. "Look, I already said I'm thankful you were there to help me with Rich. It would've been bad if he'd shifted in front of everyone. That's something we all know. I can't tell you any more than that. All I can do is ask that you don't talk about this to anyone. Please."

The look on his face had my heart stalling. He was practically begging us to drop it and not say a word to anyone. Why? Was he afraid of something? Of someone?

The Wolf Blood with the scar on his face outside Last Call floated through my mind. Was that who Teddy was afraid of?

"You do know, whatever it is you've gotten yourself involved in, we wouldn't tell anyone, right?" The words slipped past my lips before I could stop them.

Teddy's gaze locked with mine. "Just forget about tonight, okay?" He opened the door to the dormitory and slipped inside.

Holt followed him and so did I, but he was quick. He took the stairs two at a time.

"Okay, well, that was interesting," I said as I stared after him.

"Sure was." Holt scratched his neck. "I'm not sure

what we're missing, but I feel like there's a lot more going on than either of us know."

"I feel the same. Do you think Lionel was in on it too?"

Holt shook his head. "I don't think so, but I could be wrong."

"Have any theories on what they're hiding?"

"Nope. None. All I know is Teddy seemed scared of someone finding out what Rich did tonight, or what he tried to do."

I nodded. "Yeah, and I don't think it's the headmaster he's scared of."

"I don't think so either." He faced me fully. "I'm not ready to call it a night just yet. Are you?"

"Nope, my mind is spinning."

Holt flashed me a grin. "Do you like pool?"

"I've never played."

"I can teach you. It's easy. The hardest part is learning how to hold the stick, but I'm sure you'll be able to catch on quick," he said as he walked toward the pool table in the main lounge.

I arched a brow. "Was that an innuendo?"

"Only if you want it to be." He winked, and I felt butterflies burst into flight in the pit of my stomach. I loved it when he winked at me.

HOLT

A week passed. I'd been stalking Teddy, unable to get everything that happened with Rich and the awkward situation out of my head.

Something big was going on, and I was determined to figure out what.

Following Teddy had me learning things about him, and one thing for certain stuck out—he was a creature of habit. Every Tuesday, Wednesday, and Friday morning he laced up his sneakers and pounded the pavement with a morning run. Sometimes he did laps around the academy, sticking to the sidewalks and patches of grass. Others he ran through the woods. And once, I'd seen him do both.

I also learned he was in the dining hall like clockwork for every meal. He seemed to favor beef stroganoff and sloppy Joe's instead of pizza, hot dogs, or salads. Dr Pepper was his favorite soda, and peanut butter crackers were his favorite snack. He played cards with a few of the others from the house every Wednesday night. He didn't have a girlfriend. And he had a couple classes in the academic building, which let me know he wasn't just here to learn about his wolf side. He had an academic goal he was trying to achieve as well.

It was amazing the things you could learn about someone if you paid attention. You didn't even have to speak to them to learn the ins and outs of their life. All you had to do was watch.

Even so, I still didn't learn anything pertaining to that night.

Teddy never attended group meetings in the library or met in any of the workrooms for a club. He had friends, but for the most part, he kept to himself.

What was I was missing?

I tapped my pencil against my notebook, thinking. My mind circled back to the same moment it always did when I thought about this so in depth—the time in the woods. I'd been tracking Teddy as he went on one of his runs. One minute he was there, and the next, I swore he was gone. Magic had lingered in the air, warming the space between two trees. Teddy was a Wolf Bitten, though. He couldn't wield magic. Only Bounds could. This was why I thought someone else had to have met him in the woods.

Who? Rich? Someone else?

"What are you thinking about so hard over there? I know it's not Moon Phases," Tori said, shifting my attention to her. We were sitting in the library at her favorite table, which happened to be to the right of the entrance along the back wall. I wasn't sure why she enjoyed this table more than any of the others, but I was glad she did because it gave me a perfect view of not only the entrance to the library, but the entire library itself. It was because of where we sat that I was able to see Teddy as he perused the shelves of the werewolf lore section.

"Nothing," I said before glancing back to the notebook in front of me. I was supposed to be researching the sixth moon phase, and studying the previous ones, in preparation for a big exam next week, but I'd hardly written two sentences worth of notes before Teddy walked into the library and I'd glued my eyes to him like a creeper. "I've been reading, and thinking about what I'm reading."

Tori shifted in her seat to face me. We'd spent a lot of time together over the last week, but she didn't know I was still just as curious as ever about Teddy and Rich and whatever they were involved in. Teddy was easier to follow, since he was in Bitten, which was why I'd chosen to follow him over Rich. Plus, Rich seemed cocky. There was a level of arrogance around him that I didn't care for and neither did my wolf.

"Well, you better take notes on what you're reading or else you'll have to read it all over again. Just write down the key attributes of the sixth moon cycle. I remember from last semester that was what Professor Hale focused on with each phase," Tori insisted.

"Right, I forgot you took this class last semester. Here's an idea—why don't you give me your notes." I wiggled my brows. "That's a solid idea right there. I'm sure you took amazing notes. Then I wouldn't have to read all of this crap and could focus on the key points that Professor Hale will touch on instead."

Tori shook her head. "Nope. Not happening. You wouldn't gain as much if all you did was read my notes instead of the text."

I'd known she wouldn't go for it, but it hadn't hurt to ask. I leaned back in my chair and shoved the Moon Phases textbook away from me. "I'll do the reading. I'll take notes. I'll study like I'm supposed to, but it would be so much easier if you'd let me have your notes."

She gave me a playful shove and rolled her eyes. "You are such a whiny baby. I don't even know how my notes are going to help you any. It's not like I went back and circled what each test was about. They're just notes. Summaries of the chapters."

"Exactly. Summaries of the chapters. Chapters I'd rather not have to read in full."

"Doesn't it fascinate you, though?" Bewilderment danced through her eyes.

"No, not really." It didn't. Learning the moon phases only made me realize how much change my body was going through each month thanks to the wolf inside me. It was a reminder I didn't need that all of this was real.

"Moon Phases was one of my favorite classes last semester. I can't believe you don't find it even a little interesting. I thought it was cool to learn the different factors guiding our wolf through the transitions of the month."

"I don't need to learn about it when I can feel it." My

words came out harsher than I'd intended but I tacked on a slight smile to soften them.

Tori smirked at me. "Fine. I'll give you my notes."

I arched a brow. "Seriously?"

"Yep." A devious look entered her eyes, and I wondered what was going to come out of her mouth next. Excitement tingled through me. "Under one condition."

I licked my lips while holding her stare. I hoped it was something sexy. "Name it."

She leaned back in her chair and folded her arms over her chest. "I'll give you my notes if, and only if, you agree to take me to see that romantic comedy at the theater." A wicked smile twisted her lips. It was sexy as hell combined with the devilish look glinting in her eyes.

"The one with that guy I told you I can't stand?" I asked, even though I knew which movie she was talking about. Summer, Paris, and Tori had been talking about it all week.

Summer and Paris had gone last weekend, but Tori hadn't because she'd gone out with me for Mexican food and froyo instead.

Her grin grew. "That would be the one. Since tomorrow is Saturday, I figured we could go to the one o'clock showing. A day date."

I chuckled at the label she'd placed on it. Day dates seemed to be her favorite. She wasn't a night owl and studying was how she liked to spend most of her evenings.

"I thought we were going on a hike, though," I said, suddenly remembering another hike she'd found she wanted to check out. This one was supposed to have a scenic overview of the mountains, and she wanted to photograph it.

"Oh, we're still doing that, but I want to go see that movie too. This is the last weekend it's playing." She recrossed her legs beneath the table, brushing hers against mine in the process. My dick twitched at the sudden contact with her. "Do you want the notes or not?"

I shifted in my seat. "Fine. We'll go to the movie."

"Awesome."

I hated we were going to see some stupid romantic comedy, but I was excited to see Tori smile so big. She was absolutely gorgeous when she smiled.

"Since there's no need for studying now that I'm getting your notes from last semester, want to get out of here?" I stacked my notebook on top of my textbook and shoved my pencil behind my ear.

"And do what?"

I had a few things in mind we could do tonight besides study, but I'd wanted to surprise her with something all week. Now seemed like the perfect time.

"It's a surprise," I said, noticing how her smile wavered. "Just trust me, okay?"

Tori wasn't one for surprises. She'd made it clear when she flipped out on me for buying her a houseplant three days ago. I hadn't had any reason to buy it other than I thought it would be nice to give her something that would bring nature indoors for her. She was always photographing plants and animals, so I figured she might like houseplants. She'd accepted the gift, but only after some serious coaxing.

"What are you up to?" she asked. "You know I don't like surprises."

"I know. Just trust me. You're going to love it. We need to head back to the dorms, drop off our stuff, and make sure you grab your camera. You'll want to take pictures of this. I guarantee it." It was killing me not to tell her what my surprise was, but I couldn't wait to see her reaction when it was revealed.

"Okay." She licked her lips. A wide grin spread across her face, and I knew it was because I'd mentioned she should bring her camera.

"Come on. Let's go." I gathered my stuff and stood, waiting for her to do the same.

My gaze drifted to the stacks, searching for Teddy. He was no longer there. A quick glance around the library let me know he wasn't sitting at one of the tables either. He'd disappeared, but for the first time all week, I was okay with losing him. All I wanted to do was spend time with Tori.

When we stepped outside, my stomach buzzed with anticipation. The sensation intensified as we walked hand-in-hand passed the faculty and staff building toward the Bitten dorms. I couldn't help it when I glanced at the oval-shaped windows along the top of the building.

That was where I was taking her—to the tower.

She'd mentioned on multiple occasions that she wanted to get up there and take photographs of the academy grounds. From those windows, a person could see the entire campus. Who knew how far the view into the woods went.

I glanced at her, knowing she was going to be excited. She loved looking at things from different angles, and getting her up there would be the perfect way for her to take pictures of things she already had from a new angle.

I was a genius.

Also, photography wasn't just a hobby to Tori; it was her creative outlet. It kept her balanced and happy. It brought her peace. This past week each of those things had been drained from her thanks to the weight of exams. She needed a break. A moment to recharge. And frankly, so did I. I'd allowed Teddy, Rich, and the altercation that happened between them in front of Last Call to occupy my mind more than I should have. It was time to only think of Tori, and for her to refill her creative well.

Visiting the tower would be good for both of us.

At least that was the hope. Walker had been my right-hand man when it came to getting a key for the place. He'd created a crazy plan that actually worked. It involved snatching the keys from the annoying TA, Fletcher, figuring out which one was for the tower, and then making a duplicate before Fletcher realized his keys were gone. It was a crazy intense plan, one that had the ability to get us in loads of trouble, but thankfully it had all worked out. I wasn't sure how, but it had.

"Are you sure you don't want to tell me what we're doing?" Tori asked as we slipped into the Wolf Bitten dormitory behind two guys. Tori waved to a girl standing in line at the vending machine before shifting her full attention back to me. I didn't glance at her. Instead, I kept my eyes straight ahead. If I looked at her, I might cave. "Are we leaving campus? How late do you think we'll be?"

The worrywart in her was showing, and I loved it. She was cute as hell when she tried to figure things into her schedule, especially when it was something she couldn't control.

I squeezed her hand in mine, hoping to reassure her. "Don't worry about it. Just trust me and go with the flow."

TORI

 y teeth sank into my bottom lip as I tried to do as Holt asked. I wanted to just trust him and go with the flow, but I couldn't. It wasn't how I was wired. It wasn't how my mind worked. I was always in a constant state of turmoil. There were only two things in my life that ever seemed to dull it—photography and Holt.

Even though this seemed to involve both, I couldn't relax. No matter how much I wished I could.

"I'll try," I said, flashing him a small smile I hoped was believable. He seemed happy and excited about whatever it was. The least I could do was pretend to be the same.

"Good." He leaned forward and brushed his lips across mine. The slight stubble along his upper lip and jaw tickled my face. "That's all I'm asking."

I stared at him, loving the way he looked at me. How

had I ever resisted him before? Why? I had deprived myself of so many moments like this one. It saddened me.

"Let's head upstairs to drop off our stuff, then we can meet back at the top of the stairs," Holt insisted.

"Okay, but this had better be good. Not telling me where we're going has allowed my mind to wander. I've thought up some amazing things this could be; hopefully, your surprise stacks up to them," I teased.

A lopsided grin twisted his face. "Amazing things, huh?"

"Yep. Epic."

"I think I'll be fine."

I arched a brow. "Confident much?"

"Definitely."

He kissed me on the forehead before moving to start up the staircase. I kept pace beside him, my heart forcefully beating in my chest. What could he possibly have planned for us that he thought was so good? Where were we going? Was it within walking distance, or would we be driving? My wolf paced, the feel of my unease bleeding into her brain as well. She was just as uncomfortable as I was. I pulled in a deep, steady breath, but it did little to calm either of us.

"See you in a few minutes. Don't forget your camera," Holt said once we reached the top of the steps. He released my hand and disappeared through the door that led to the boys' dorms. I headed to the girls' side, my mind racing with what his plans might be.

I couldn't figure it out. It couldn't be the movie I wanted to go see, because he'd already agreed to see that tomorrow. Plus, he'd also said I needed to bring my camera. A hike was out too, because we were already scheduled to do one in the morning.

I grabbed my ID card from my back pocket and slid it into the door of my dorm. When I opened the door, Summer was at the desk, eating a bag of Twizzlers while watching something on her phone.

"Hey," she said without looking up from her cell as I closed the door behind me. "Did you two finish studying so soon? I figured you guys would be down there all night with exams next week."

"Yeah. I thought we would have been too, but it's okay. I still have time to go over everything once or twice before the test," I said as I headed to the closet for my favorite camera and to change into a thicker sweater. The temperature had dipped already. Since I didn't know where we were going, I figured changing might be a good idea. After I pulled the sweater on, I grabbed my camera.

"Heading out to take some pictures? I haven't seen you do that all week," Summer said as I attached my most comfortable strap to my camera. I didn't know if we'd be walking a lot wherever Holt was taking me, and this one would ensure I didn't have a crazy rash on the back of my neck by the time I got home. "You okay? It's rare that I see you reach for your camera on a Friday night unless something is bothering you. The academy getting to you? Or is it Holt? Are you two having problems?"

Her questions came at me like rapid-fire. How much sugar had she consumed today? Knowing Summer, that could possibly be her second bag of Twizzlers today.

"I'm fine. Holt said I needed to bring my camera. There's someplace he wants to take me tonight. It's a surprise," I said as I slipped my camera over my neck. I grabbed a hair tie next, and twisted my hair on top of my head.

Summer's eyes glittered. "A surprise?"

"Yup." I allowed the P to pop, showing my disdain.

"Doesn't he know how much you hate surprises?"

"I told him, but he still wouldn't fill me in on where he was taking me tonight. He told me to trust him and go with the flow."

Summer laughed. "I'm sorry. I don't mean to laugh, because I'm sure this has you all kinds of stressed, but he has a lot of learning to do when it comes to you and going with the flow."

I frowned. "Yeah, well."

"Girl, you know I love you. It's just that going with the flow really isn't your cup of tea. Like at all," Summer said once she was able to contain her laughter. "Surprises are not your thing. I'm sure this is driving you nuts and I'm sort of glad. Maybe it will force you out of your comfort zone."

"Oh, I'm feeling nuts, but not in the way I normally would. It's weird." I moved to glance at myself in the mirror behind the door. "I can't explain it, but I'm not as worked up as I normally would be. I'm pretty sure it's because of Holt."

"Aw, you two are so sweet." Summer took a bite of her licorice strand. "I'm glad you gave him a chance. Also, I can tell you're falling for him."

My face heated due to the way she grinned at me. "I'm not falling for him. It's too soon for all that."

"Lies. All lies," she insisted. "You're falling for him. He's falling for you. You're going to live a happy life together and make loads of cute babies."

"Whoa there. No baby talk, please. We haven't even slept together yet."

"You will tonight." She winked before taking another bite of her licorice strand. "I'm sure he has someplace awesome planned to take you to tonight so you can finally do the deed. Hope you shaved your legs this morning," she said in a sing-song voice.

"That's not how tonight is going to go."

Was it? Well, even if it did, the good news was that I had shaved my legs this morning. Thank God.

"Stop resisting him. Holt is sexy as all get out, and you know you want him. Let it happen," she said. "And don't worry, I won't be waiting up for you. I have plans of my own to get laid tonight. After I learn how to do this kickass braid." She waved her phone in the air.

I rolled my eyes, but laughed. Summer was a trip. "I'll see you later."

"And when you do, I expect all the juicy details of the night."

"Promise." I swiped my Chapstick from on top of my dresser and applied a layer before heading out the door to meet Holt.

As soon as I stepped through the door to the girls' dorms, I spotted him. His hands were shoved into the front pockets of his jeans and a boyish grin twisted his lips when he looked at me. Butterflies burst into flight through my stomach as Summer's words about doing the deed tonight rushed through my mind.

I knew right then that was exactly what was going to happen and that I was ready.

"You remembered your camera. Good," he said. His eyes skimmed over the length of me. "I'm glad you changed into a sweater, too. I didn't think about what the temperature might be where we're going. I'd hate for you to freeze."

"I'm sure you would've found ways to keep me warm." The words had sounded better in my head. Way sexier. Out loud, they just sounded awkward. My face grew hot. I risked a glance at Holt, gauging how he'd taken what I'd said.

He wore a shocked expression, but it melted quickly as a pleased one took its place. "Oh, absolutely."

I played with a strap on my camera and rolled my ankles unsure of what I should follow up with saying. "So, can you tell me where we're going yet?"

Not the best, but it would at least steer the conversation elsewhere. I was not good at trying to be sexy. It felt too forced and awkward, and I was positive it came off exactly that.

"Nope. Not gonna happen." He held a hand out to me, and I slipped mine in it, lacing our fingers together. It was the most natural feeling in the world. His hand was warmer than mine, but it felt like heaven. "You'll find out soon enough."

We started down the stairs, making our way outside.

Holt steered me in the direction of the faculty and staff building. I didn't ask where we were going again. Instead, I decided to trust him and roll with it, like he'd asked previously.

At least until we stopped in front of the double doors to the faculty and staff building.

"What are we doing here?" I asked, unable to help myself.

"Like I said, just trust me and roll with it."

He motioned for me to step inside first. I did, but I made sure to glance around while doing so. Were we even supposed to be in here? I hoped we didn't come face-to-face with any teachers or staff members. They would definitely wonder what the heck we were doing in here on a Friday night, same as I did.

Holt headed to the staircase dead ahead, but I pulled his arm, jerking him to a standstill.

"Where are you going? We can't go up there," I hissed, not wanting anyone to hear me.

He flashed me a wicked smile and pointed to the ceiling. "We're going up."

Up? Oh my gosh, he was taking me to the tower!

I'd said more than once that I wanted to go up there. From the height and the position of its windows, I'd be able to photograph the entire academy. I was giddy with excitement at the thought.

"The tower?" I asked, praying he said yes.

"That would be the surprise."

I fought the desire to release a scream. "How are we going to get up there? And when we do, how are we going to get inside? I'm sure the door to that area is kept locked."

Holt reached in his pocket and pulled out a key. He dangled in front of my face. "With this."

How the heck had he gotten that? The question burned on the tip of my tongue, but I didn't ask because of the sexy smirk twisting his lips. It said that I needed to trust him and roll with it, yet again. When Holt started walking, so did I. Nerves twisted through my stomach as worry we would run into one of our professors, the head-master, or any member of the faculty or staff and be asked what we were doing.

I hoped he had a good lie already picked out in case because I had nothing.

When we made it up two flights of stairs, Holt grabbed my waist and pulled me to a stop. I let out a gasp and then looked up at him. He placed his index finger to his lips, letting me know I needed to be quiet. My heart hammered as I glanced around, trying to figure out what he'd heard that I hadn't.

Heels.

They clicked on the stairs above us, coming in our direction. My eyes bugged out as I glanced back at Holt again. He looked calm. I didn't know how, though.

We were about to be busted.

The sound of the heels grew closer. I licked my lips, my legs trembling beneath me as my mind raced with reasons for why we might be here to give. A cell phone rang, echoing through the stairwell. Holt pulled me to the right. I didn't resist, hoping he had crafted a plan that might stop us from being found because, as much as I wanted to head to the tower and take some photographs, my desire to not get into trouble was greater.

Holt pulled me behind a leather sitting chair and motioned for me to crouch down. I did while thinking to myself how crazy it was that fear had blinded me from spotting the hiding spot myself. It was genius, especially since the woman had answered her phone and seemed to be in a heated conversation with someone. She'd most likely be too distracted to notice the two of us crouching behind the sitting chairs in the small landing area.

At least that was the hope.

"And, what do I always tell you? I feel like we have had this conversation on multiple occasions and you still don't seem to comprehend you shouldn't come to me with these matters. There's a certain pecking order," the woman said in an irritated tone as she continued past us down the stairs. "What happened with Mathias is being taken care of. His trial will be in a few weeks. I don't need to tell you any details beyond that." There was a pause as someone else spoke. "Yes, Lionel will still be attending the academy. You leave that to me. I feel he will easily come to our side. He talked to his father. That was what we wanted. Now he's been awoken to the truth. So has his girlfriend, Miss Mayor. Things are shaping up. We've just had a few mishaps here or there. The resistance has been craftier than we gave them credit for; that much is clear."

Her last words were barely audible considering the amount of distance between us and the force she slammed her heels against the marble staircase with, but both Holt and I were able to distinguish what she'd said. We waited a few more heartbeats before slipping out from behind the chairs and resuming our trek to the tower.

"Lionel? As in Lionel Daniels?" I asked in a hushed tone once I figured she was far enough away.

"I don't know, but I can't think of any other Lionels that I know. It's not a super popular name."

I continued to jog up the stairs as quietly as I could beside Holt. "You're right. It's not. Plus, I'm pretty sure Gloria Mayor is in Bound too. I had a class with her last semester. She's in my lunch this semester, and I am ninety-nine percent sure she and Lionel are a couple."

"What do you think she was talking about when she said he's been awoken to the truth?" Holt asked, casting a quick glance at me.

"No clue, but it brought up thoughts of what happened in front of Last Call between Teddy and Rich," I said.

"Do you think Rich is part of the resistance she was talking about? The one that was giving them a few mishaps? And who are they?" Holt sounded confused.

I glanced at him. His brows were pinched together. It was clear he was working through things in his mind, trying to fit pieces of a puzzle together. I left him to his thoughts as we continued to climb the stairs. We were close to the top of the tower; we had to be.

"There have to be two groups. I think that's what's going on here," Holt said, surprising me. He glanced at me, and I spotted excitement shifting through his eyes. It was clear he'd worked through something in his head and was trying to share whatever it was with me, but I was lost. "Two opposing groups."

"Opposing groups to what though?" I asked as we started up what looked like the final flight of stairs.

Holt ran a hand through his hair. "I'm not exactly sure, but from her conversation, we now know that one of the groups is called the resistance. I don't know what they're resisting, but I'm willing to bet it has something to do with Rich wanting to reveal himself to everyone, even the humans, at Last Call."

"So, one of the groups might be about revealing our true nature to the humans, while the other might be about resisting or opposing it?" I asked, not with the intention of humoring him, but with the intention of trying to figure out what this big breakthrough he felt he'd stumbled upon was.

"Exactly." Holt paused at the top of the staircase and dug in his pocket to retrieve the key for the tower door. "Why would a group of wolves want to reveal themselves in the first place? And if they did, and they had a good reason for it, why would there be a group forming to go against them? It seems like Lunar Academy holds even more secrets than any of us bargained for."

My mind bogged down trying to follow his train of thought. "You could say that again."

Holt sighed. "Let's not worry about that right now," he said as he inserted the key into the door to the tower. "Let's focus on this." He winked before turning the key. The sound of the lock falling away echoed through the narrow stairway we stood in. Giddiness flooded my system. "Ready to get those pictures you've been dreaming about?"

"Absolutely!"

Holt swung the door open and motioned for me to step through. "Ladies first."

I wasted no time walking through the threshold and into the tower. The air was stale, lukewarm from the fading sun, and smelled musty. There was a hint of something else lingering in the air, but I couldn't pinpoint what. I felt around for a light switch, wanting to see the room completely.

"I can't find the light switch," I said. My fingers continued to feel along the place where I thought one should be.

A loud crack from beside me captured my attention, and seconds later, the room filled with an eerie green glow.

"Wow, that's stealthy and ninja-like of you. Where the heck did you get a glow stick from?" I asked once I realized what he held.

"Convenience," he said, naming the only gas station in Brentwood. "I figured it would be best to use something like this instead of the flashlights on our phones or the actual light to the tower. It might draw less attention."

I smirked at him. "You don't think a green glowing light coming from the tower isn't going to draw any attention?"

Holt shrugged. "I didn't say that. I just said that it

might draw less attention. Maybe whoever sees it will think it's a professor up here, performing magic for next week's lesson."

His theory made sense. It also had me wondering if the odd scent mixed with the musk in the air was the lingering residue of magic. "Hmm, maybe."

"Aren't you going to look around?" Holt asked. The air of satisfaction about him made my smirk turn into a wide smile. "Maybe take some pictures? We did come up here for a reason."

My teeth sank into my bottom lip as I tore my eyes away from him. While the glow stick he held didn't offer much light, I was still able to make out the space perfectly. The ceilings were tall. The windows were narrow, arched, and nearly ran from the floor to the ceiling. I was in love with every aspect of the tower, right down to the weathered wooden floors.

"It's beautiful," I said in awe as my gaze continued to bounce around.

"It's empty."

I blinked. He was right. There wasn't a single piece of furniture in the entire room. Nothing. While this wasn't necessarily an odd thing, the lack of dust and cobwebs was. It hinted that this space was used frequently, but for what?

A shiver slipped along my spine. I stepped to the nearest window in the hopes of pausing my overactive imagination about the things that might go down here away. The window was drafty, but that was to be expected out of one so old. My gaze drifted out the window and across the campus.

"You can see everything from up here," I said. The quad. The winding road that led to the academy. The bushes and small garden. Students coming and going, oblivious to me watching them. You could even see the edge of the woods along the property. "It's amazing."

I lifted my camera and started snapping shots, capturing the view. There wasn't much light left in the sky, but I angled myself and my camera just right to take advantage of what little remained. Photography was all about the right angle and using the light available to you.

Holt moved to stand behind me. I could feel the heat of his body pressing against my backside. Energy pulsed between us, charging the inches remaining between us. My breath hitched at the feel of it. I struggled to regulate my breathing, knowing he'd most likely taken notice to its change. Thank goodness it was dark in here, because my face was flaming with my embarrassment from the way my body had reacted to his sudden close proximity. Even my wolf had nipped at me for it.

She liked Holt. She wanted him. But she didn't want me to make a fool of myself.

"It is a pretty amazing view," he whispered in a husky tone still standing behind me. Did he know how sexy his voice was? Was he trying to turn me on? "I'm glad you enjoyed coming up here as much as you thought you would."

"I am. Definitely. Thanks for bringing me up here." My voice quivered when I spoke. He was so close. I knew all it would take was for me to turn around and stand on the tips of my toes, then our mouths would be together. That kiss would lead to something more, though. I could feel it in the charged air between us. Was I ready for that? I'd thought I was earlier. "I know you probably went through a lot to make this happen, and I want you to know that I appreciate it. This is the perfect surprise."

I took a risk and shifted to face him. The hint of a smile curved at the corners of his mouth. I stared at his lips longer than I should. My breathing grew shallow, and my entire body tingled to life at the sight of his tongue snaking out to moisten his lips as I continued to stare. Unable to control myself any longer, I let my camera dangle from the strap around my neck and lifted to the tips of my toes to crush my mouth against his. His hands gripped my hips, his fingers digging into my skin, and I knew this was what he'd been waiting for. I arched my body toward him at the feel of his tongue sliding against my bottom lip, teasing my mouth for entrance.

My wolf panted with her need for him. Heck, I panted with need for him. Right then, I was so damn thankful I'd shaved my legs because Summer had been right about how the night would unfold.

Tingles spread through my lower extremities as I bit down on Holt's bottom lip, nibbling with that fiery need burning through my core. Holt didn't seem to mind. Instead, he hoisted me into the air, forcing my legs to wrap around his waist. He walked us to the center of the room where he gently lay me on the floor of the tower and then positioned himself above me. Our lips only parted so he could remove my camera from around my neck and lay it beside us.

I lifted his shirt to place my hands against the heated skin of his back, needing to feel him. His muscles were flexed as he held himself above me with his arms, and as I trailed my nails down the length of his back, goose bumps prickled across his skin. A moan escaped him, and I swore it was the best sound I'd ever heard. When he tugged the collar of his shirt and slipped out of it, I gave into the sticky heat of passion swirling around us and lifted so I could peel out of my shirt as well. Holt unhooked my bra and tossed it to the side. His mouth dipped to my pebbled nipples, causing spasms of pleasure to rock through me from the sensation. I unbuttoned his jeans, fueled by my desire to feel him—all of him. At the sound of his zipper releasing he paused what he was doing, and we locked eyes.

"Are you sure you're okay with this? We can stop if you're not," he said. The look on his face made it clear he didn't want to stop any more than I did, but that he would if I said I wanted to. He was a gentleman, and for whatever reason, this turned me on even more.

"I don't want to stop. I'm good." I reached into his pants and stroked him to further prove my point. Holt moaned, and then crushed his lips against mine in our most fiery kiss yet.

HOLT

J was floating on cloud nine. So much so, that I couldn't wipe the smile off my face no matter how hard I tried. Sex with Tori had been mind-blowing. Amazing. Fantastic. Perfect. It was everything I'd thought it would be and more. The best part was, she seemed to have enjoyed herself as much as I had. The smile that refused to leave my face was mirrored on hers, and I felt like a damn king because of it.

"Well, that was unexpected," I said as I buttoned my jeans and then zipped my fly.

She narrowed her eyes, but her smile never fell away. "Was it? You can't tell me you didn't have intentions of getting me up here with you just so we could do that."

"I didn't," I said. She arched a single brow. "Well, maybe a little. I mean, I hoped. A guy can hope, right?"

"Of course. And don't worry, I'm only teasing you. Sex was on my mind when I came up here too," she admitted.

While I couldn't see if her cheeks had turned pink with embarrassment due to the green glow of my glow stick, I didn't need to. I could sense it. I erased the minimal amount of distance between us and pulled her close, gripping her hips. When she refused to lock eyes with me, I hooked my finger beneath her chin and lifted her stare to mine.

"There's nothing wrong with that," I said before brushing my lips across hers. "In fact, I think it's sexy when a woman knows what she wants."

"You do?"

"Absolutely."

"In that case, I want a repeat of that sometime soon." A wicked smile that had me wanting to strip her naked and pleasure her all over again twisted her lips.

"That can be arranged." I moved to kiss her again, but the sound of movement coming from the other side of the tower door caught my attention. "Shit. We must've been louder than I thought."

The door swung open before I could think of what we should do, and Teddy, Bryant, Rich, and the TA, Fletcher, stepped into the room. I positioned myself in front of Tori, blocking her from everyone's view even though she was already fully dressed. It was a protective gesture that came to me on instinct thanks to my wolf. He didn't like the aggressive way these four had barged in.

Frankly, neither did I.

It was clear from the look on Fletcher's face that they weren't surprised to see us. This put my wolf on edge even more. He snapped and scratched at the surface of my mind, wanting to take over because he felt threatened by their presence.

"I think it's time we talked," Fletcher said. He clasped his hands behind his back and stepped farther into the room. I took a step back, forcing Tori backward with me. I didn't know him well, and therefore that meant I didn't know what he was capable of. "You seem to be incredibly curious. And you know what they say about curiosity."

"What do you want with us?" I asked, not willing to play games.

"The same could be asked of you," Fletcher insisted. Bryant closed the door behind them as they all stepped farther into the room, and my heart stalled inside my chest. Shit. This wasn't good. "You seem to want something from us. Teddy specifically. Answers maybe?"

My gaze drifted to Teddy. Sympathy festered in his eyes. It was clear he wasn't going to be any help to us with whatever was about to go down. I looked to Bryant next. During fight club, he seemed like a decent guy, but now I wasn't so sure about his character. Maybe I wasn't as good at reading people as I'd thought. Neither was my wolf. Both of us felt dumbfounded at his presence in this situation.

"Rich, do your thing," Fletcher said without looking back at him.

Rich stood beside Teddy, his arms folded over his chest. Irritation was reflected in his eyes. I licked my lips, waiting for what would happen next.

Was he about to charge at me? Use magic against me?

When he lifted his hands in front of him, palms facing up, and the sharp scent of magic filtered to my nose, I reached for my wolf. If Rich was going to use magic against me, the only way I had a chance of going against him would be if I shifted. I hoped Tori took advantage of the distraction and got herself out of here.

"Run." I tossed the word over my shoulder to her seconds before I morphed into my wolf.

She listened, but didn't make it far. Bryant grabbed her, jolting her to a standstill. My wolf growled and snapped at him, letting him know that he needed to let her go.

He did, surprising me.

"Calm down." Bryant grinned. "I'm not going to hurt her, but she needs to hear this, just like you."

"You were right about him," Fletcher said, nodding to me before shifting his attention to Bryant. "He is a time bomb. He thinks with his wolf and not his head."

Rich muttered something and made a movement with his hands. Lights came on in the room, illuminating it in a soft glow.

"He's hostile, yes," Bryant said. "But, I think if he was filled in on things, that would dissipate enough for him to become an asset. He needs a purpose. A cause. Something to focus on besides how fucked up his life is now that he's been bitten."

My wolf cocked his head. If I'd been in human form still, I would have done the same. How did Bryant know my inner workings so well? Everything he'd said seemed to strike a chord in me.

"I don't know. We're not trying to start a war, and I think that's exactly what he would provoke. He's not what we're looking for," Fletcher said before he shifted his attention to Tori. "Her, on the other hand, how did she manage to slip through our fingers? You're perfect for what we aim to achieve." His eyes flashed as he stepped closer to her.

My wolf growled, and Fletcher paused.

"And, what is it exactly you're trying to achieve?" Tori asked. Her voice was steady and clear when she spoke. Her stance was wide, and she was prepared to fight should the need arise.

She wouldn't reach her wolf; I knew this after everything she admitted to me previously about being afraid, but I knew she wouldn't go down without a fight either. Neither of us would. Come hell or high water, we were getting out of here.

Alive and together.

My gaze bounced between Bryant and Rich. I wasn't sure who presented a bigger threat, but knew they were the two who needed to be taken out first if we were to survive this. Whatever *this* was.

"Where to start, where to start," Fletcher said as he paced the length of the tower. My wolf focused on him. "Hidden among the students, faculty, and staff of this fine establishment are members of an ancient organization. We are called the Elite, and we are made up of individuals from the first of our kind all the way down to those of your generation. It's quite impressive, actually."

"What do you want?" Tori asked, surprising me. She

clearly was on the same level as me and didn't give a shit about a history lesson on ancient organizations.

"I think you already know what we want thanks to Rich." Fletcher glanced over his shoulder at him. Rich gave a shrug.

"I let my anger get the best of me. It happens. Look at Holt." He motioned to me.

My wolf growled at him. This wasn't me letting my anger get the best of me, shifting happened to be the only way I felt I had a chance to protect Tori and myself from the four of them.

"To reveal yourselves? That's what you want?" Tori insisted.

"Smart girl," Fletcher said with a smug smirk.

Tori folded her arms over her chest and shifted on her feet. I remained at her side, watching each of them and looking for the right moment to attack. "Why do you think I would help you achieve this?"

"Because of your past, of course. Your upbringing," Fletcher insisted. His eyes were intense as he stared at her. "You were raised by one from Bitten and one from Born. You chose this life; you chose to be bitten. You're the perfect example of humans being accepting of our kind."

While that might be true, I'd be damned if I let them force her to do something she didn't want. My wolf tensed, ready to pounce should anyone try to touch her.

"Is that why you're trying to come out? Why you're revealing yourselves? You want the humans to accept us?" Tori asked. Her tone drew me to look at her. Her expression was soft and hope glimmered in her eyes. "Is there a chance they would? Humans typically fear what they don't understand."

"Typically." Fletcher began pacing again. "However, you were accepting."

Tori's hands flew up. The movement startled my wolf. She glanced at me before shifting her attention back to Fletcher. "I was also a child. They were my parents. They adopted me. Children are often more accepting than adults."

"This is true, but in today's society, adults have opened their minds more so than they have in the past. They are accepting of a multitude of things, as they should be, and we believe they will be accepting of us. However, there is a group forming who doesn't share our beliefs. Not entirely."

"Should we be telling them so much?" Bryant asked.

Fletcher's eyes shifted between Tori and me, lingering on her longer. "I'm confident these two will join our regime. As you said before, that one needs a cause, a purpose, something to strive for. Joining us would give him exactly that. He would be part of a new age. The dawn of a new era. And this one, she will be the glimmer of hope we need. She's proof that what we're striving for can be achieved," he insisted. "Two nights from now, the Elite meet. I would like the two of you to attend that meeting. You will be introduced to our leader and some members of the group and can decide then whether you want to join us."

"And, if we don't?" Tori asked. It was exactly what I'd been thinking.

"No harm, no foul." Fletcher waved his hand as a devious smirk twisted his lips.

I didn't trust him, and I damn sure didn't believe him.

Without another word, he turned and left the tower with the others following him. Tori and I were left alone with our thoughts, and the room was so quiet you could hear a pin drop.

TORI

The next two days passed slowly. I'd been on pins and needles, waiting for members from the Elite to abduct me for their meeting. It was possible I'd seen one too many thriller movies, and my overactive imagination had been running wild because of it.

Out of the two of us, I was the only one who seemed nervous about the situation. Holt seemed fine.

"You okay?" he asked. His thumb made lazy circles along the back of my hand. "You look like you drifted away for a minute on me."

I gave his hand a gentle squeeze and flashed him a smile. I had drifted away. My mind hadn't been my own the last two days. It tended to wander and daydream more frequently than ever before.

"I'm fine. Just trying to think of how tonight is going to go," I insisted.

Holt leaned against the pillows on my bed. It was a little after eight, and we were sitting in my dorm, waiting for the sun to go down. Summer left us almost an hour ago, claiming we were making her feel like a third wheel even though we hadn't been doing anything besides listening to music and talking. However, I was glad she'd left. It had been hard the last couple of days keeping this secret from her, and I was too nervous now that the time was approaching to keep up my act.

My walls were crumbling.

"Have you decided yet?" Holt asked. The song on the app we were streaming music from changed to something haunting, sending an ominous vibe through my room.

I tucked a few stray hairs behind my ear and met his stare. "Actually, I think I have."

It had taken me both days, but last night I had a dream that pointed me in the right direction with my answer. It was the sign I'd been praying for. At least, that was what I was taking it as. I'd always believed dreams held deep meanings we should listen to.

In my dream, our kind stepped from the shadows and revealed ourselves in the most peaceful and calm way to the humans—to the world—and everything was beautiful. Everyone was accepting and loving, and it wasn't long before the other breeds of the supernatural races decided to step forward from the shadows too. We were the first, but we weren't the only ones, and there was beauty in that.

I took it as a sign that this was something I was supposed to be part of, something I was supposed to do. And while I still woke up with nervous butterflies fluttering through my stomach and anxiety stealing my breath at times, I felt fairly confident I was making the right decision for myself.

"I'm joining," I said.

"You are?" There was no judgment in his eyes or hostility. His question came from a place of shock. Apparently, joining the Elite wasn't something he thought I would do.

I licked my lips, my eyes never leaving his. "Yeah, I think it's the right decision for me. I liked what Fletcher said about me being the perfect example of humans and wolves coexisting. I think it's something everyone should experience the same as I think it's something everyone should have the choice of. I know it wouldn't stop others from being bitten in horrible ways, but I do think situations like those would dwindle if people were given the opportunity to become bitten on their own. I also think everyone would be happier if we came out. Life would be better. There wouldn't be any hiding or fear of being found out. I feel good about this. And I have to just go with my gut on it."

As I spoke, my anxiety and nervousness melted away. There was a strength inside me that pushed through that I hadn't known was hiding. It came from believing what I was saying wholeheartedly. It also helped that the dream played through my mind while I spoke as well, reassuring me and bringing with it all the emotions I'd felt from it.

"I'm glad you're joining," Holt said. "I am too. Bryant was right when he said I need a cause. A purpose. I need some sort of direction. Every plan I ever made for myself was scrapped because being bitten changed everything.

This will give me the sense of direction I've been needing, a cause and purpose." He lifted my hand to his mouth and placed a kiss to the back of my knuckles. "Everything sort of feels like it's finally all falling into place. I think I'd be dumb if I turned my back on this opportunity to be a part of something."

My cell alarm went off, ending our conversation as we both stared at my phone.

"I guess it's time to go meet the members of the Elite and let them know we're joining," Holt said.

I tapped my phone, turning off the alarm I'd set so we wouldn't be late. "Yeah, let's go." My voice was steady, and surprisingly my nerves didn't come back like I'd thought they would.

Maybe it had something to do with the fact that Holt and I were on the same page. I could do anything with him at my side. He gave me strength. I liked to think that I did the same for him too.

"We've got this," he said. "I think we're making the right decision."

I nodded and then stood. "I think so, too."

Holt unplugged his phone from my charging station and disconnected it from my tiny speaker before stepping to the door. I jotted down a note for Summer, letting her know not to wait up for me, and placed it on her pillow.

"Ready?" Holt asked with excitement glimmering in his eyes.

"Ready as I'll ever be," I said.

When we made it down the stairs and outside the Bitten dormitory, I pulled in a deep breath to steady my hammering heart. It didn't do much good, but the feel of Holt's hand in mine seconds later did. We walked to the edge of the woods and stepped behind a big tree where we were supposed to meet Bryant. He was the one who'd given a message to Holt about the meeting place and time earlier in the day. While the guy unsettled me, he didn't unsettle my wolf. Was I too focused on his scar and the intimidation he always seemed to radiate to actually see him for who he was, I liked to think that wasn't the case, but there was a possibility it was. Heck, it could even be because he was from Wolf Blood, and I hated to admit it, but they always freaked me out. It was the whole being part vampire thing.

"You made it," Bryant said. He peeled himself off the tree he'd been leaning against while waiting for us.

"You had doubts?" Holt teased. I didn't know why, but it seemed as though the two were more comfortable around each other than they should be given the fact they were from separate houses and didn't seem to have a single thing in common.

Bryant returned Holt's grin. "Not in the slightest." He nodded toward the woods. "Follow me."

Holt squeezed my hand twice before we followed Bryant through the thick foliage, disappearing into the woods.

Doubt crept through me the deeper into the forest we went. I wondered if it was such a good idea to follow someone who left me so uneasy deep into the woods in the middle of the night without letting anyone know where I was or what I was doing. My parents would kill me for being so stupid. Anxiety squeezed my lungs as thoughts of being chopped into tiny pieces by Bryant floated through my mind.

"Breathe. You're okay. Trust me," Holt whispered against my ear.

I forced my lungs to pull in a breath, hold it for the count of three, and then release it slow and steady. "And roll with it," I said, repeating the words Holt had said multiple times the other night.

"Exactly." He winked.

Bryant came to a complete standstill and shifted to face us. I thought he was going to say something about my nerves, but he didn't. Instead, he reached for the edge of his shirt and pulled it over his head, revealing his incredibly muscular body. I averted my eyes and felt my cheeks flush.

What the hell was he doing?

"Strip. It's time to shift. The others are waiting for us," Bryant said.

Shivers slipped up my spine at the mention of others waiting for us somewhere in the words. My gaze drifted to search the shadows, but I didn't see anyone. My wolf didn't seem to sense anyone either.

When Holt released my hand and began to undress, I assumed he figured all must be well and I did the same. I folded my clothes into a neat pile on top of my shoes, trying to ignore how awkward and embarrassing it was to be naked in the middle of the woods with two guys. I didn't think I'd ever get used to the lack of issues wolves had surrounding nudity.

Shifter energy stung my nose, and I glanced at Bryant. In seconds, he was a dark wolf with yellow eyes and an exceptionally large form.

"Trust me, and roll with it," Holt said before he shifted as well.

My teeth sank into my bottom lip as my wolf attempted to force her way to the surface. The scent of shifter magic had caught her attention unlike anything else. It had been since the last full moon, when the academy hosted a sanctioned run, that we had shifted. Which was how it was supposed to be. This was an unsanctioned run. It was against the rules. Nevertheless, I held my breath as I gave way to my wolf. She was gentle yet firm as she took over. We'd learned a lot together during our time at the academy, and even though I was still uneasy about giving her control, she did everything she could to reassure me in this moment.

Soon, the three of us were running through the woods nearly in a single file line, dodging trees, sticks, and low-growing foliage. The strength, speed, and muscle of my wolf never ceased to amaze me. She was graceful yet strong. Fearless yet beautiful. She was enjoying herself, even with the situation at hand.

I tried to tap into her calm. Just when I thought I had, my wolf picked up the scent of others nearby and my anxiety came back full-fledged.

It wasn't long before we ran up on two wolves and a guy. I didn't know who the guy was, but it was clear from the look of him he was a student at the academy. He looked too young not to be.

My thoughts scattered when one of the wolves standing beside him nipped at his leg. As though the guy could read the wolf's mind, he unclasped his hands in front of him and lifted his palms to the sky. Green light outlined in purple built in his palms. It shot out, hitting between two trees beside him. I was mesmerized by the color as it danced between the trees, illuminating the entire area. Magic caressed against my wolf's fur, causing her to tense. It was then that I realized what was going on, and what I had stepped into.

Another broken academy rule. No magic was supposed to be used outside of the classrooms. Not unless it was supervised by a professor.

This kid was no professor, but I imagined that either of the wolves could be. This didn't make me feel any better about the situation, though. The purple and green lights faded into a foggy mist, leaving the only light shining on the area coming from the sliver of moon above. The same wolf that snapped at the guy before, snapped at him again.

"I know what I'm doing. We talked about this multiple times. Don't worry. No one else will get through. We're good, just go," the guy said, his deep tone vibrating through the air.

No one else would get through to where? Did he just open a portal?

The two wolves standing at his side looked to Bryant before turning and starting through the thick mist that seemed to be growing denser by the second. They passed between the two trees where the green and purple lights had lit up the area seconds before without looking back again. Bryant followed them, then Holt, and then me.

Once I stepped between the trees, it was clear I was no longer in the same forest as before. It looked the same. Trees, shrubs, low-growing foliage, mountains in the distance. But it didn't feel the same. Maybe it was all in my head. I couldn't be sure. However, when Holt looked at me, I knew it was because he felt the same.

"Here they are," a familiar voice said.

I tore my eyes away from Holt and glanced to the clearing we'd come to. People and wolves stood staring at us as we grew closer. Fletcher stood among them. There were a few other faces I recognized in the crowd, but I couldn't focus on them. All I could focus on was the man standing in the center. Dominance radiated off him unlike any wolf I'd ever met. His face was stern, yet his eyes were warm and welcoming. Authority shimmered off him into the air surrounding us, but it didn't deter me from stepping closer.

"Jackie," the man said, his tone oozing that same level of authority.

A girl I'd seen before around campus stepped forward. A pile of robes rested in her hands. She held them out and flashed Holt and me a smile, but I could sense the unease flickering through her. She was trying to please the man by doing as he asked, but she seemed on edge. I imagined it was because she didn't trust easy.

"Please, return to your human form. The robes are there in case you would like one. We all know not everyone, especially those from Wolf Bitten, are as okay with nudity as some of us others," the man said. I expected him to smile, but he didn't. Instead, he shifted his gaze between Holt and me.

My wolf was reluctant to let go, but she understood I would set her free again on the way back. My heart hammered as I reached for one of the robes Jackie held out. After I slipped it on, I secured the belt around my waist. Holt did the same and then stepped to my side. His hand rested against the small of my back, and I leaned into his touch, drawing strength from it.

"I trust Fletcher has filled you in on who we are and what we stand for," the man said, wasting no time with pleasantries. "Do you have any questions?"

"We heard Fletcher's definition of what you stand for, but I think I speak for us both when I ask for you to give yours," Holt insisted, surprising me.

Back in my dorm, he'd seemed so certain joining the Elite was a good thing, but I wondered if our trek through the woods and the use of unsupervised magic, as well as the size of this group, gave him doubts. Either that or he was being cautious, which I didn't think was a bad thing.

The man smirked at Holt and nodded as if in approval of his question. "Very well. We are called the Elite. We're made up of some of the most ancient of our kind as well as the newest. We don't discriminate against any house. We are all about preservation of our kind."

"And you hope to do that through revealing yourselves to the humans? To the world?" I asked, unable to keep quiet any longer.

The man's gaze shifted to me. I stared into his eyes.

While I had been right in assessing that they were warm and welcoming even from a distance, now that I was closer, I could see how ancient and full of wisdom they were as well. This man was an old soul.

Was he one of the ancients he mentioned?

"Yes. We believe humankind has reached a generation where they are more accepting, tolerant, and willing to coexist with us. We feel the time has come to walk out from the shadows and live our lives to the fullest. Without hiding. Without fear. With nothing besides peace and love."

I tried not to laugh at how much he sounded like a hippie. Even so, what he sounded like was coinciding with my dream and signifying to me yet again this was where I was needed.

"Now my question to you is: Will you join us?" the man asked us.

Holt shifted beside me and I glanced up at him. His eyes locked with mine, and in them I found his answer still remained the same, as did mine.

"Yes, we will," Holt answered for the both of us.

The man nodded, and again I felt as though it was in approval. "Wise choice."

His words hung suspended in the air, causing me to wonder what would've happened if we had declined their invitation.

"Step forward," the man insisted. He held out a hand, waiting for someone to put something in it. When Fletcher handed him a silver dagger with intricate designs carved into the handle and blade, I felt my throat close up. "Each of you, hold out a hand so that I may complete the initiation rite."

Holt took a step forward and then held out his hand palm up like the man asked. I was more hesitant, the thought of having a blade slash across my palm didn't seem fun. Still, I stepped forward anyway. When I did, I noticed everyone around us—those in wolf form as well as those in human form—bowed as the man positioned himself in front of us.

"It is better to end your life with this dagger than to join the Elite with doubt in your heart. How do you enter?" the man asked me.

What I was supposed to say? What words was he looking for? Nobody had briefed us on this part. My heart hammered as time ticked away. I thought back over my reasoning for why I'd decided to join in the first place. I pictured my mom and dad. I pictured what it had been like growing up as their child. I pictured how happy I had been even knowing what they were. How loving and accepting we had been of each other. Minus Grandma Myrtle.

"I enter doubtless," I said, knowing it was the right thing to say.

The same look of approval shifted through the man's eyes before he sliced the blade across my palm. I winced at the sudden pain, and warmth trickled from the open cut, spilling onto the forest floor. I didn't jerk away, though. I didn't even flinch. There was something in his eyes that told me not to.

He shifted his attention to Holt next and asked him

the same. He was faster in his response than I was when he replied, "Doubtless," and then the blade was drawn across his palm too. The man brought the dagger to his own palm next, cutting it open as he had ours. He shifted to me and pressed his palm to mine. We stood frozen, open wound to open wound, for a few heartbeats before he moved to do the same to Holt.

"By oath and blood, I welcome you to the Elite," the man said.

A chorus of claps, cheers, and howls exploded around us. My lips twisted into a wide smile as a sense of peace settled over me. Holt pulled me close, and I leaned into him, knowing this was exactly where I was supposed to be—where we were supposed to be.

THANK YOU

Thank you for reading *Wolf Bitten*. We hope you enjoyed it! Look for more Lunar Academy stories to come soon.

STAY UP TO DATE WITH THE AUTHORS:

Find out more about us online:

Visit Alyssa at https://www.alyssaroseivy.com
Stay up to date on Alyssa's new releases: ARI New Release Newsletter.
To see a complete list of Alyssa's books, please visit: http://www.alyssaroseivy.com/book-list-faq/

Visit Jennifer at https://jennifersnyderbooks.com
Stay up to date on Jennifer's new releases: Jennifer's Newsletter
To see a complete list of Jennifer's books please visit: https://jennifersnyderbooks.com/book-list/

Also, please consider leaving an honest review at your point of purchase. Reviews help us in so many ways!